DAHLIA SEASON

DAHLIA SEASON

stories & a novella

MYRIAM GURBA

(a Future Tense book)

Manic D Press
San Francisco

For TJ

The author would like to thank the following publications where some of these stories originally appeared, in slightly different form: *Tough Girls* (Black Books), *Bottoms Up* (Soft Skull), and *Problem Child* magazine.

The *Future Tense* series is edited by Kevin Sampsell.

Cover photo: © Cora Reed. www.corachaos.net
Author photo: © Ivana Ford. www.ivanaford.com

Library of Congress Cataloging-in-Publication Data

Gurba, Myriam.
  Dahlia season : stories & a novella / Myriam Gurba.
    p. cm. ~ (The future tense series)
  ISBN-13: 978-1-933149-16-5 (trade pbk. original : alk. paper)
  ISBN-10: 1-933149-16-7 (alk. paper)
  1. Mexican American lesbians~Fiction. 2. Goth culture
(Subculture)~Fiction 3. Identity (Philosophical concept)~Fiction.
4. California, Southern~Fiction. I. Title.
PS3607.U5485D34 2007
813'.6~dc22
                                        2007010565

Contents

stories

Cruising

The beach is really crowded today. Somebody has their radio tuned to the oldies station and they're playing "Tell It Like It Is." It sounds sad. It's too hot for a song like that. It's the hottest day Long Beach has had in a really long time and they say it's going to break records. Out in the street it looks like there are puddles but it's just mini-mirages from the heat. The same thing on the pier. You wanna watch for those puddles you might slip in but it's really just the heat.

Long Beach is not a clean beach. It's crowded and full of trash, like Styrofoam cups and plastic wrappers and soda cans. Long Beach is also a poor beach. There's no blondes in bikinis or movie stars. That's Malibu or Orange County. This is a real California beach. Everybody here is Mexican or maybe Filipino or Black. There are all kinds of Mexican kids out splashing in the water. Some of their moms are old gangsters. They're the big ladies parked on the faded beach blankets. You can tell what they are—veteranas, old-time gangsters—from their sloppy tattoos. There are no waves today but some of the little boys have their boogie boards out anyway. They're grinning and they're just floating, kind of going back and forth to the lazy rhythm of the ocean.

The pier is covered in people. Two drunks are having a burping contest and if you go anywhere near them you can smell the cheap malt liquor that they keep chugging out of their 40s. Brown paper bags wrap their bottles but hide nothing, the burps reek like King Cobra and are so loud you can hear them halfway down the pier. It's gross. It stinks like fish up here, too, and people are fishing right where the kids are swimming and I wonder if anyone ever gets hooked by accident. Some kid could get it right through the skin but nobody seems to care. There are a million lines in the water and they overlap. They look like spiderwebs.

To my left there's a little Mexican boy baiting an anchovy on a rusty hook. Next to him this little cholo has an octopus in a bucket and his kid brother is poking it with a stick. It's going to die soon. To my right there's a dark-skinned punk boy on a plastic chair that's too small for him, probably from Pic'n'Save. He's trying to act cool, ignoring his family, his jefita, his mamá who's passing out sandwiches wrapped in tinfoil to his brothers and sisters. He's too cool to be kicking it at the pier with his family but they probably told him he had to go and it's so hot out that he figured why not. His hair is in great big spikes, pointy, and they're going to melt because of the heat. He looks like his heart is covered in barnacles and he'd rather be anywhere but here.

To escape from the sun, a lot of people crowd under the pier. It's like there's a little city down there trying to stay cool. There's all kinds of people down there—families, fags, lovers, bums, drunks—everybody huddled under the pier trying to get wet and avoid sun. That's their common bond. That and they're not rich people, not the kind of California people you see in movies but the real kind of people who live and breathe and sweat and die in California.

This is the pier that separates the good beach from the poor beach. The good beach is about a mile down on the other side and it's called Belmont Shores. That's where the white people go. It's right on the tip of Orange County. The beach that I'm on, that the pier belongs to, is the brown beach. The water is murky and weird stuff washes ashore all the time. About fifteen years ago they found something really horrible on the beach here. It was a head, just a head. No body, no hands, no nothing. This homo serial killer had cut it off one of his tricks but nobody knew that at the time. It was just a John Doe head until they found out Randy Kraft had been hunting and killing fags here in Long Beach for years, preying on boy whores, barflies, and even a few Marines.

At night, the fags like to fuck under the pier. I come out here with my friends sometimes and get drunk at night and listen to waves, and the pier looks like a scene out of a John Rechy novel, all sorts of hot clandestine fucking. You can see silhouettes moving back and forth to a really provocative rhythm and you think they'd just go to the gay bars down the street and have sex in the bathroom or the alleys. Broadway is right next to the beach and it's lined with gay bars but for some reason these guys like to do it old fashioned, cruising outdoors.

It's dangerous what they're doing and maybe they're closeted or they haven't even come out to themselves. They probably don't know that this was Randy Kraft's old hunting ground. The beach patrol comes by at night to scare them and the straight couples who get it into their heads that it would be romantic to have sex on the beach away. They're especially tough on the fags. They'll drive across the sand in their little jeep and this guy'll get on his loudspeaker and he'll yell into it, "Okay, faggots, pull up your pants. The party's over." You can see the shadows stop, their rhythm breaking and they scatter like roaches. But they're back again within a couple of hours.

The Queen Mary is docked nearby. It's one of the city's biggest attractions. Right now they're auditioning monsters for the haunted boat show that they have every year at Halloween. They decorate the boat all creepy and it costs twenty bucks to get on and see the show. They say that the boat really is haunted. There are things floating through it, walking the halls. The Spruce Goose used to be parked in a hangar nearby and some people say that Howard Hughes' ghost wanders around it. You can hear his footsteps clicking and clacking against the bare concrete floor.

In the 1940s, Long Beach was really different and it had this fun boardwalk where sailors and Navy men used to hang out. It was kind of like Santa Monica with a wooden roller coaster and lots of games with cheap prizes. The air smelled like hot dogs and sweet cotton candy and kids could have fun for not a whole lot of money because there was a penny arcade with a big carousel. But the boardwalk had plenty of things for grown-ups, too. Because of the port, sailors would go hang out at the boardwalk before they had to ship out. It was always full of uniformed men, Navy boys in their little white pants and cocked gobs rolling up their sleeves to get tattoos of hearts that said "Mother" or their girl's name. The boardwalk was also lined with bars that were dark and smoky inside and there were girls everywhere looking to make a little money off of the sailors who might not be seeing women again for a very long time.

There was a really weird little wax museum at the end of the boardwalk that got famous for this gross exhibit they had there. It was run by some evangelical Christians who wanted to put a stop to all the vice they thought was destroying the boardwalk so they made these wax displays of what venereal disease did to the body. There were wax penises and wax vaginas with syphilis and the clap to scare the sailors away from fast sex and whores. But instead of scaring the sailors, they would get drunk or smoke some weed and then go to the museum and trip out on the wax replicas and laugh until their sides ached.

They say the Black Dahlia—this really, really famous murder victim—used to hang out there. She had a taste for sailors and servicemen and tattoos, and she combined these loves by hitching up her black dress and biting her lower lip and letting an inkslinger buzz some fella's name into her thigh. No one's certain what was written on her leg cause when her severed body was found in an empty lot, the banner was gouged out of her flesh. The killer might've been jealous of some other guy's mark on his victim's body, but I like to think it was the fiend's John Hancock, a clue too precious to abandon.

The Black Dahlia's old haunts are gone now. The roller coaster, the bars, the tattoo parlors. The only thing that's still there is the carousel. The faggot sailors that started cruising the boardwalk back then, in the '40s, opened it up for the faggots who do it now. See, Long Beach is a city full of fags, working class fags. Short bears, sober queens, anarchist punk boys who like to suck dick. There's a lot of dykes here too because they can afford to live here. It's not like West Hollywood where you can't make it on an average dyke's salary. There aren't many trannies though. Way more trannies in Hollywood. But I hate Hollywood.

The bathrooms at the beach are the best place to go cruising. I go sometimes. At first I just watched but now I do it, too. The first time I went, it was with my friend Stan. He took me to the Tomkat, this fag "theatre" on Santa Monica Boulevard, and he disguised me as a boy. I just put on really baggy pants and put up my hair in a beanie with a ball cap on over that and wore a big puffy jacket. I had on boots. I looked like a baby-faced Mexican boy. We went and sat down in the dark and after a while Stan got up and left me there. This guy came and sat down next to me. He took out his dick and jerked himself off. He looked kind of like Paul Reubens. Maybe he was. I sat and watched but I didn't touch him. I could've if I'd wanted to.

I've cruised this beach at night before, under the moonlight. I wear the same kind of clothes, everything all baggy and loose and my hair up in a Yankees cap. The first time I went alone, I almost turned back and went home until I saw this Mexican guy looking me up and down. Now, girls check each other out like that all the time but it doesn't mean anything. Girls do it because we're trained to check out other girls. But when a guy looks at you like that it means something totally different, it means only one thing. So I followed him down to the beach. He took the stairs and he held onto the handrail. It was really cold that night and the air smelled like dead fish. We didn't say anything. We just walked.

The beach felt like a different place at night, like a place full of dangerous possibilities that the waves were whispering to me. The guy had walked on ahead and I saw him turn into a public bathroom. I followed him there and stood outside for a second. I put my hands in my pockets and listened to the tide. Then I walked into the boy's room that smelled like pee-pee and seaweed. There were already three other guys in there. One was standing with his back to me with his dick out, just holding it there like he was waiting to go pee. The other was leaning against a stall, just sort of watching everything. The Mexican guy was squatting with both feet on the toilet, sort of checking everybody out. This dude had a moustache and looked sort of wetback, like he probably had a wife or at least a girlfriend. The wetback was checking me out. His hair was kind of long and he was short.

More faggots started showing up and it made me nervous. There were six of us in the bathroom. Everybody kept taking out their dicks or rubbing their crotches so I went and stood next to a urinal and touched myself over my pants. The wetback checked me out as I did this and I know that if I'd been packing what he wanted I could have gone over to him to get a blowjob. I wasn't though so I just stood there sort of squeezing myself like the other guys and then I saw someone I liked. He was a white guy, kind of younger, dressed sort of plain, kind of emo. He looked kind of lost but he was definitely queer.I looked right into his eyes but he looked down at the floor real fast. He was in there only a few minutes and then he was gone.

When I noticed he was gone, I went outside to go find him. He was standing by himself, smoking over by the girl's bathroom. I saw the cherry of his cigarette bobbing up and down, and he was wearing a white T-shirt so he wasn't hard to see. I walked over to where he was standing and just kind of leaned against the wall. We were quiet. He was blond. He walked over to me and sort of stood there smoking. He finished his cigarette and then he dropped it into the sand. His face slowly came at mine and he kissed me. His mouth tasted good, dirty and boyish, and his cheeks scratched my face. It was good to kiss a boy. He kissed me hard, his tongue darting around hot in my mouth like a wet warm lollipop and he sucked my lips. It was lovely.

He kissed me like that for a little while and then he pulled away. He grabbed my ass and he squeezed it. He felt it and he slipped his hands down my pants through my boxer shorts. He felt my hips. He kissed me and he reached down to grab my cock but he felt my wetness and I opened my eyes and he opened his. His finger was on my pussy and I pushed him away. I started running and I didn't turn around. I ran up the stairs that led up the cliffs to the sidewalks and walked the rest of the way home. I got to my apartment and slipped the key into the door. I fell asleep in my boy drag and when I woke up the next morning I could still taste the emo boy in my mouth. But he was gone. I had spoiled everything. I ruined it by being myself, by being a girl.

Just Drift

No Mexican celebration is complete without a flan. I needed one bad, but not for no party. I needed a dessert to avoid my own funeral. I was going to bribe a powerful, plus-size woman with it.

Operación Flan began with my big sister, Lydia. She's famous for two things, being a phenomenal bitch and being a good cook. Last night, she got home from the bank all tired but, I begged her, I mean down on my hands and knees begged her, to make me one of her legendary desserts.

"Lydiaaaaaa," I moaned, "you have to make me one. If there was a flan category in the L.A. County Fair, the judges would give you the blue ribbon, for sure!"

"Get off the floor, idiot! You look pathetic! Why does your skinny ass need a damn flan anyways?"

Lydia's bad attitude got the better of me. "None of your damn business! Just do it!"

"Forget you!"

I got off the floor and brought out the big guns: "Remember that grocery money you stole from Mommy's purse last year? She still doesn't know you took it and gave it to your old boyfriend, Tommy, the one Mommy hated more than all the rest."

"You little bitch," Lydia seethed. "You wouldn't?"

I smiled and nodded. Lydia stalked into the kitchen and got busy.

I breathed a sigh of relief and walked to my bedroom and sat at my desk, switched on my computer. The piece of shit's always freezing, so I prayed to the virgin for no technical trouble, cracked my knuckles and began typing my junior thesis, "Catch-22: A Gay Romance Novel." On page nine, my cell rang. It vibrated like a pair of chattering teeth off my desk and onto the carpet. Not wanting to disrupt my flow, I let voicemail get it.

Twenty pages later, it was midnight. Yossarian, the world's biggest closet case, was getting on my last nerve so I bullshitted my conclusion, did a fast "Works Cited" list and title page, and hit "Print." My thesis popped out. I stapled it and slid it into my backpack.

My cell vibrated so I leaned over and picked it up off the carpet. 1 New Message blinked on the display. I dialed voicemail and put the phone to my ear. Sokhun's voice demanded, "Cassidy, be under the mural of Bill the Buffalo at seven-thirty, sharp."

Sokhun. She's my girl, my vieja[1], what old time homeboys would call my heine[2], a title that sounds like highness. Sokhun's tiny and Cambodian with long, straight, silky black hair and she complains her name's common, like the Khmer "Jennifer," but to me, it's gorgeous. What do I know though? Love blinds me. I'm the puppy in one of them

---

1   old lady
2   Mexican ghetto slang for chick

what I think they call "spring-fall relationships." Sokhun's a senior. I'm barely a junior.

I called Sokhun back, but her phone rang and rang. With my cell still in hand, I leaned back on my mattress, shut my eyes and crashed hard as the space shuttle falling back to planet Earth.

Because of being blackmailed into cooking, Lydia woke up grouchy this morning. Esa ruca[3] was stomping around the apartment and she hates me regardless. Lydia's jealous cause I'm prettier than her; I got all the looks in this familia[4]. Plus Lydia thinks I'm a loser cause my crappy grades got me "d"-moted from Advanced Placement classes to almost all regular ones.

I don't care I ain't with the smart kids no more; all's I care about is kickin' it wit' my girl, listening to my iPod, and DRIFTING! Vroom-vroom-vroom! Lydia thinks she's the shit cause she's leasing a German car and studying to be an accountant and she wears a suit to work everyday and stands behind bulletproof glass wondering how fast she can fill a sack with money if a guy wearing pantyhose over his head shows up in her teller line.

"Caaaaaaassidy!" Lydia shrieked at six thirty. She pounded on my door with her fists. "You best be ready soon or I'm leaving yo' ass!"

My eyes popped open. No blur, everything was clear cause I'd forgotten to take off my glasses. I was dressed in yesterday's wrinkled clothes, too. I bolted upright. "Hold your frickin' horses!" I yelled. "At least let me take a shit!" I got up and walked across the hall to the bathroom and slammed the door shut.

"I'm leaving!" Lydia yelled.

"Hold up, bitch!"

'Bitch' drove La Shrieker over the edge. "So that's how it is?" she yelled. "Then let the Long Beach Public Transit system be yo' fuckin'

3   That hag
4   family

18

chariot to school!"

I heard the front door slam shut so I pulled up my pants, ran out of the bathroom, grabbed my backpack off my floor, and the flan out of the fridge. I booked it out of our apartment, down the stairwell and through the lobby door just in time to see Satan's white Jetta making a right down 43rd.

At times like these, all you can say is fuck it. So I said, "Fuck it." I straightened my glasses and fixed my backpack straps and my necklace and ran my hand across the foil covering the flan. Luckily, it was unharmed.

I hiked the two blocks to the bus stop and sat on the uncomfortable, homeless-proof bench and waited and waited. The 90S finally pulled up and I climbed aboard thinking, "Now we're jammin'!" and jinxed myself big time. I heard the beep of the wheelchair ramp being lowered. Gazing over my left shoulder, I saw an old white dude with sausage stumps for legs being lifted parallel to the floor. Flush with it, he pushed a red button on his electric chair and whizzed over to the front seats with the blue handicapped sticker above them.

The bus driver came and collapsed them and folded them flat and I sat down and watched her strap the guy in so he wouldn't jostle like crapshooter's dice. The lady used fingers tipped by the longest acrylics I've ever seen to adjust the cords and buckles and belts and these nails were gold with diamonds set into crescent shapes at the ends. Decorations like that should be against public transit rules. Those claws have got to make it hard to grip the wheel and them gemstones could accidentally catch the light and blind oncoming traffic. *Dazzle...Screeeeech...Ka-Boom!*

With the legless wonder secured nice and tight, the hawk-woman got back behind the wheel and got the show on the road, rolling us up Sands Boulevard, toward the ocean. I swear, a passenger dinged the bell to get off at each and every stop: St. Luke's Hospital, the Salvation

Army, McDonald's, this pinche[5] ride was taking forever, and I yanked the string two blocks up from Delightful Donut, my palms slippery with sweat cause it was hot and I was positive I was late.

I stood to peer out the window to check who was hanging out at the donut shop. White and Mexican straightedge nerds crowd the outdoor tables around seven, plot vegetarian takeovers of the cafeteria, and leave by seven forty-five. Old Cambodian men with coffee and dominoes replace them at eight and if their game's hot, it means you're late for school.

At a pink table, I saw an old Asian guy with his legs crossed like a chick. Another guy sat across from him and he held a black domino in the air above a tile configuration that formed a T-shape. He set his tile down, making the tail slightly longer, but the domino T still seemed real short. Maybe it wasn't eight yet.

The bus stopped and I staggered to the front and grabbed a pole for balance. "S'cuse me, miss," I said to the driver. "Do you know what time it is?"

She flipped her skinny purple braids, tapped her nails against the wheel, and looked at the fake Roley on her wrist. "Eight oh five," she answered. "Time to get yo' ass to school. Bell already rung at Willmore."

"Oh, shit! Thanks!"

Gripping my flan, I flew down the bus stairs, landed on the corner, and almost got hit by a car sprinting through the crosswalk against red. A horn honked at me and I ran past the 98¢-and-Up store, across a little two-lane street, hopping onto the curb and dashing across the lawn in front of the auditorium. I darted into a pine tree cluster and peeked around a trunk to check the scrolling marquee left of Will's main entrance. It looks like a gigantic cell phone broadcasting text messages to everyone driving down Sands.

---

5   fucking

70°. 8:08.

Shit.

I looked to my right, at the thick chains wrapping around the white gate. They confirmed my lateness. I weighed my options. I could walk back around the auditorium, past the music building and the overflow bungalows to the track. There, I could hop the chainlink fence, sneak in, and play it cool. However, this production would put the flan in serious jeopardy. It probably wouldn't survive the climb, and I absolutely couldn't afford to leave it behind.

I picked to play it safe and go in through the side door. Sighing, I hung my head and plodded across the dewy grass, to the cafeteria, around the corner, up the narrow sidewalk along Buffalo Drive. It's a tiny street that leads into the teachers' lot and cuts past the Industrial Arts wing, dead-ending at the baseball diamond. The Buffalo Drive door is the only legal way of getting onto campus late and approaching it, I fronted like I was more of a bad ass than I really am.

I worried that my nervousness showed as I joined the thrashing blob of latecomers. I glanced at the doorway. It was a human toilet clogged by fuck-ups and retards waiting to be processed by Will's finest: the racially ambiguous bald security guard everyone calls Vin Diesel; Amanda, the girl security guard who everyone says is Rosie O'Donnell's Samoan cousin; and Mr. Reyes, the Hispanic vice principal who looks like Mr. Clean.

I stood casually between some members of the A-Team, this gang of vicious Asian skate punks, and the E-Z Writers, a crew of Latino taggers. I thought, "I'm chill, I'm chill. I'm inconspicuous."

"Wassup, Cassidy?" this girl tagger, Pixel, asked me.

"Oh, you know," I said. "I'm late. Huh, huh, huh."

"Listen up!" Vin Diesel shouted. Everyone quieted down. "Let's make this easier on ourselves, people! Those with a note from Mom or Dad clearing them and who've got school ID, step forward."

A short black girl and a short white girl stepped up.

"Shaneeka Martin and..."

"Kimberly Krantz."

"Come on through," Vin ushered. Mr. Reyes handed the two girls pink hall passes. "The rest of the ladies, follow Amanda. Gentlemen, Mr. Reyes!"

A runt-sized tagger whined, "Man, this shit is whack!"

"It's bound to get more whack if you don't shut your mouth," Mr. Reyes told him.

The tiny graffiti artist clammed up.

Mr. Reyes marched us in through Buffalo Drive's puke-colored doors, leading us through a dim hallway that emptied into the sunlight. We followed him across the asphalt past a snack bar, the boys' gym, the girls' gym, the pool, the nurse's office, and the overflow classrooms. That's where I should've been, in a stuffy bungalow with my last fancy class, Honors English. Instead, I was being herded with a bunch of miscreants up a flight of stairs to the second story of the 900 building.

Mr. Reyes unlocked a dented brown door with "OCTS" stenciled on it. He held it open. "On-campus Tardy Suspension, gentlemen. Have a seat."

Kids poured in ahead of me and staked out all the good seats in the back. I walked to a leftover desk in the third row and slid into the plastic chair. Mr. Reyes entered last and walked over to the beat-up wood-paneled desk at the front of the room.

"You all know the drill," he said. "Three of these," he pointed at the blackboard, where "OCTS" was written in chalk, "and you get real suspensions. Looking at your faces, I know this is some of your thirds."

Mr. Reyes smoothed his pink tie. He sat at the desk and produced an expensive ink pen from his shirt pocket. His silver hoop earrings jiggled. "Isidore Washington...," he started and he confirmed our names and grades and who our guidance counselors are and he wrote everything down on a pad of legal paper attached to his clipboard. After he called my name, Roberto Cassidy Moran, I twiddled my thumbs in silence for, like, ten minutes. Then, I remembered the flan.

I raised my hand. Mr. Reyes didn't notice. He was busy reading the LA Times travel section. Maybe he was planning a vacation.

"Mr. Reyes?" I said.

He lowered his paper and looked at me. "Yes?"

"I brought this special flan, and it has to be refrigerated. Can I take it somewhere to be refrigerated? Please?"

The black walkie-talkie clipped to Mr. Reyes' waist crackled. Everyone leaned forward to listen. Sometimes, you can hear the longshoremen down at the docks cussing up a storm on certain frequencies.

"I'll take it," Mr. Reyes said. He held out his hand and I picked up the plate and brought it to him.

"Now, it's really good flan, Mr. Reyes," I joked. "Try to resist the temptation. Okay?"

He looked at me and didn't say anything. I could tell from his eyes, though, that his brain was taking my name and repeating it silently as an insult: Moron. God, I hate being a Moran!

I shoved my hands in my sweatshirt pockets and spun around and walked back to my chair. Mr. Reyes left and locked the door behind him, trapping us like Jack and Rose in Titanic. The only way out was through the windows. In the event of a disaster, we could die.

I put my head on my desk and looked at everyone's feet. I counted and did the math. Of the twenty pairs of feet in the room, 75% were wearing Vans. Some had on Authentics, the super-traditional kind that the O.G. skaters from Dogtown made famous. Other kids had on Old Skools with stripes going down the sides. All the rest had on slip-ons. Camo slip-ons. Jolly Roger slip-ons. Checked slip-ons. Pink hippopotami slip-ons. So on and so forth. Since everyone at this dang school's a conformist with their Vans, I wear Etnies.

"Cht, cht," I heard. That's a sound nacos, ghetto Mexicans, make to get someone's attention. "Cht, cht. Coconut. Hey you. Brown on the outside, white on the inside."

I looked up. Two dumb cholos, the Mexican Laurel and Hardy, were sitting in the fourth row, grinning at me. The fat one had on blue Authentics. The skinny one wore Chucks. Both pendejos[6] were styling it old school, like a couple of throwbacks to *American Me* in starched khakis and buttoned up plaid shirts.

"I ain't no coconut, foo'," I said to Humpty.

"You ain't? Check it out. Little faggot haircut. Thick black glasses. A fuckin' shell on your necklace. Tight sweatshirt with an eagle on it from like the Gap or some shit like that. Your get-up be lookin' pretty white and gay to me."

"I think the Twinkies have gone to your head," I told him. His skinny friend laughed.

"You bangin' on me, homes?"

"Tsk, whatever."

"Shee-yit. You best shut yo' mouth right now cause you bangin' on a Loco!" Fattie threw the gang sign for E.S.L., Earth Shattering Locos.

"English as a Second Language?"

The thin friend giggled more and fatso's nostrils flared and his jaw clenched. "Better watch it, coconut, cause I'm-a be lookin' for you. And when I find you, I'm jackin' yo' flan!" He high-fived his anorexic friend.

Losers.

I put my head back down, ignored them, and shut my eyes, letting my imagination do what it usually does during downtime: become my personal car factory. I zoned out of OCTS as my head built and

---

6   Dummies

customized me a winner's drift machine, a shiny candy-cane Nissan Silvia S15, manual transmission all the way, baby, shocking red bucket seats to fall into. When they were done, my crack team of Japanese engineers dressed in white lab coats pushed my ride out onto the wet streets of Tokyo at midnight. Dr. Fukuyama held the door open and I slid behind the wheel. I gripped the clutch and reached out to touch the windshield made of glass so shiny and crystal clear, I wouldn't have believed it myself if I hadn't touched it.

Fans, mostly Harajuku girls, packed the city sidewalks and Sokhun stood with them, dressed in a red kimono, looking like a geisha. I revved my engine for her and she waved, and I rolled down my window and some hoochie-mama with bleached hair and short shorts screamed, "Ichi, ni, san, shi, GOOOOOO!" and I gunned it, leaving my competition—a vicious yakuza boss and Japan's prime minister—in the dust. I entered a blind turn full throttle, oversteering big time cause that's drifting, doing too much, too fast, too soon to lose traction, riding up on two wheels but still managing to make the rear of your vehicle follow your...

Beeeeeeeeeeeeeeeeeeep!

Nope, that wasn't my horn or the yakuza's or Junichiro Koizumi's. None of us, like, died in my imaginary car race or whatever. The interruption was real. The shutdown bell. It sounds during emergencies and when teachers hear it, for our protection, they're supposed to lock us into our classrooms and not let us leave and close all the windows and blinds.

Last year, we had a shutdown during World History. We were studying the Battle of Britain and our teacher, Mr. Schwarz, had us pretend we were in an air raid, hiding in a London subway station while Nazis and R.A.F. did aerial battle above our city. Really, what happened was some white kid freaked out during a random bag search in the main quad, where the rose garden and flagpole are. The kid was acting suspicious, and instead of giving himself up, which would've been the easy thing to do, the stupid white boy took off waving a handgun in the air. The staff and police found him under the bleachers in the football field after, like, two hours of looking, and they bragged to the local paper that they averted a mini-Columbine.

Liars. I think that white boy was probably really like that nerd on *The Breakfast Club* who got an F in Woodshop cause when he pulled the trunk or tail or whatever on his elephant lamp, the light wouldn't turn on. The lame ass was probably planning on taking his gun into the bathroom and shooting himself in order to make a big scene and be remembered when nobody knew his frickin' name anyways.

I sighed and sat up and opened my eyes and unzipped my backpack to get my phone out. I wanted to text Sokhun about being trapped in OCTS and ask her if she knew what was up. Reaching inside my JanSport, I felt around. No phone. I peered inside. It was all shadows but I clearly saw the outline of my hairbrush and a pack of gum. I took them out. I lifted my backpack and turned it upside down and shook it slow and watched my junior thesis, a copy of *Super Street* magazine, my iPod, and a pair of tangled-up earphones slide out. No phone.

"Gosh dangit!"

The cholos started to laugh.

"Shut up, fuckers!"

They got quiet. Pussies. They must not have been real gangsters.

A Black kid got out his Nextel. "Monique," he chirped. "This C'Love. Why we under lockdown?"

"My teacher say they found a big-ass puddle of blood in the bathroom at the girls' gym but no body," her soft voice answered.

"Ugh," C-Love moaned, grossed out. "Thanks. I'll chirp ya later."

With the mystery solved and no way of making contact with my girl and my drifting fantasy dead, I started untangling my earphones. I picked out the knots and slipped the phones in my ears and stuck the plug in my iPod. Turning it on, I hit "shuffle" and rested my head on the desk. I listened to Echo and the Bunnymen, Depeche Mode, The Smiths, Joy Division. Some new stuff came on, too, like The Editors, The Postal Service, and Tegan and Sara, but the retro tunes were really predominating the mix.

After about seventeen songs, I looked up at the clock. 9:30, time for Nutrition, our fifteen-minute break. We weren't getting it today. Sighing, I dug a marker out of my backpack and lifted my head back up. Graffiti covered my desk. I read it and thought about what to add to it, what would go well with the rest of the stuff. There were Crip tags, a little E-Z Writer mural, a cross-out of ESL and the word "killa" written beside it, a random "Live to die, dying to live." I uncapped my marker and chewed on the end, thinking. Then I wrote, "Dream as if you'll live forever... drift as though you'll die today." The edges of the desk were clean, virgin, so I tagged "Kuchi, kuchi, kuchi, kuchi, kuchi..." all around. "Kuchi" means "mouth" in Japanese.

I noticed a flurry of activity so I looked up and everyone was putting away their sidekicks and PSPs and Nextels so I ripped out my earphones and shoved everything into my backpack. Someone had heard the key in the lock and warned everyone. Sure enough, the door opened and Mr. Reyes walked in, holding a bullhorn. He posed in front of us like a boot camp sergeant.

"I'm sure all of you know what's up by now," he said. "If any of you gentlemen know who the source of all that blood in the girls' gymnasium restroom is, come forward and tell someone. Think of someone you trust and let them know what's going on. Someone's badly hurt and needs medical attention. Now, the bell's gonna ring in a second. Remember, today's an odd day so go directly to your third period block. Cassidy, come by my office at lunch so you can pick up your flan."

"Yessir."

Beeeeeeeeeeeeeeeeeeeep!

Everyone bolted outta there like jackrabbits hearing a shotgun blast.

In the hall, I looked around to see if I couldn't locate any of Sokhun's friends. Her first period class is on the other side of campus but I wanted to give one of them the message that I didn't have my phone with me. I stood in the same spot for a couple of minutes but didn't see anyone. I turned and headed back down the stairs, through the bungalows, into the main building where the principal's office is. I took a shortcut through the attendance office and came out in the quad.

Mr. Reyes was standing by the yellow roses, shouting through his bullhorn, "Move it, move it, move it! You've got three minutes left to get to class on time!"

Like a V.C. navigating the jungle, I moved through the sloppy throng of kids, past the flowerbeds and the dying lawn, making it to the 400 building, walking in through the heavy side doors on my way to Mrs. Kiku's. She's my Japanese teacher, pardon me, my sensei, and I'm in her Level Two class.

Right now, Mrs. Kiku's walls give me a headache. She's got layers of our work stretching all the way back to September covering every inch of space, bright menus we made for a food project called "Arigato Cafe," posters we did for "Profile: Japan" and "Tokyo at Night," origami cranes, boxes and bats and lotuses we made with wild paper all hung from what look like laundry lines crisscrossing the room a few inches above our heads. It's enough to make a kid epileptic but in spite of the anarchy, I really do like her class. It's cool learning Katakana and Hiragana and about Japanese culture. My favorite's when we get to play with the plastic sushi Mrs. Kiku keeps in her file cabinets. I pretend to eat unagi and throw my voice like the eel is saying its final goodbye and sounding like Elmo from *Sesame Street*, it goes, "Sayonara, guys!"

The final bell rang, and I breathed easy; my homework wasn't due till Friday. Half the class, though, last names A through L, had to perform theirs. They were going to give "How-to" presentations about an activity of their choice. We had two weeks to prepare them and the talks were going to take all period. Procrastinators were wigging out, putting the finishing touches on their half-assed projects, looking at the relaxed suck-ups with jealousy. I leaned forward and wriggled out of my sweatshirt and hung it on the back of my chair. Waiting for Mrs. Kiku to finish roll call, I leaned over, picked a paperclip off the floor, and unbent it. Using the sharp end, I scratched "Just Drift" into my desk. That's what I plan on doing my presentation on, drift racing. I think Mrs. Kiku will like it. The motor sport got its start in Japan.

"Konichiwa!" Mrs. Kiku said.

"Konichiwa, Sensei!"

"Abel Andres," Mrs. Kiku called, and the choont[7] walked up to the podium and everyone cracked up all through his presentation, "How to Make Tamales," because there's no Japanese word for "tamales" and it sounded funny, all that Japanese with "tamales" thrown in over and over. Shayla Arrington went next and did hers on playing tennis. That's how most of the talks went, just instructions on how to play a sport or make a food or do household chores. Shayla brought in a tennis racket and tennis balls and wore her tennis skirt because Mrs. Kiku explained that those of us who brought in props would get one extra credit point per prop. Henry Wilson, who did how to bake a cake, practically brought in a shopping cart full of ingredients. I'll bet he raised his grade from an F to at least a D.

Best presenter was Dantrell Jackson. He did "How to Krump Dance." He brought in the DVD *Rize* to show the king of krump, Tommy the Clown who lives in Compton, and Dantrell also showed us a video of himself competing in and winning a krump battle. The

---

7   Mexican country bumpkin

crowning moment came when he got Mrs. Kiku to stand beside him to try to learn how to pop her booty, like a stripper. She couldn't master the move but she was a good sport about it.

After Dantrell, this short little lesbian whose name I can't remember but who looks like an anime character did "How to Change a Tire." She brought a wrench and a dirty tire and some lug nuts but she apologized, "I can't show you the crowbar part 'cause the principal took my crowbar away."

Dantrell asked, "You brought a crowbar to school?"

She grinned and nodded.

Dantrell was impressed. "That's vicious!"

Mrs. Kiku tossed the lesbian two points for the missing crowbar. She believes in A's for effort.

The class kiss-ass, Daisy Lara, went last. She did "How To Get an A in Japanese, Level 2." Someone coughed, "Bitch," at the end of her presentation. With everyone done, we clapped and whistled, and Mrs. Kiku told us "Sayonara," and the lunch bell rang.

"Sayonara," I told her as I walked out the door and headed in the direction of the main building. I maneuvered my way through the quad, this time dodging lines of starving kids waiting to buy pizza at carts operated by short ladies with hairnets. I entered the main building by the trophy case and went straight to the office. It was pretty empty.

"Hi, Mrs. Ruiz," I told the school secretary. She was drinking Diet Coke. She set the can down on her desk.

"Hi, Cassidy."

"Could you please get Mr. Reyes for me?"

"Sure. He just finished suspending someone but I'm pretty sure he's not doing anything now." Mrs. Ruiz got up and walked to Mr. Reyes' door. She knocked.

He opened. "Yes?"

"Cassidy Moran is here to see you."

He poked his head out. "You want your flan back?"

I nodded.

He turned and opened a mini-fridge by his desk and got it out. "Here," he said.

I walked around the counter and took the plate from him. "Thanks."

"No more tardies. Okay, Moran?"

"Alright. Thanks again, Mr. Reyes."

I turned and left and headed out the side door, going south, to the hot, dusty bungalow maze most people avoid at lunch. I arrived at my English teacher, Ms. Valdez's, classroom, and walked up her carpeted ramp. She was sitting at her desk grading papers, smacking gum with her mouth open.

Ms. Valdez is my favorite teacher. She's a Mexican greaser girl, or I should say, lady, with chunky Bettie Page bangs and pin-up girl tattoos on her forearms. She dresses nice, more fashionable than most teachers and full-figured women, and she always wears bright red lipstick that makes her look paler than she really is. Because she's weird and cusses, she's one of the most popular teachers at Will.

On the wall behind her desk, she's got a shrine dedicated to Morrissey, and on her desk, she's got what she calls her "natural history museum," a lacquered alligator head with glass eyes, a baby shark in a jar, a paperweight of a frozen scorpion. Mounted on the wall above her phone, there's a taxidermied pheasant. She introduced him to us on the first day of school.

"Class, I'd like you to meet Seymore," she said.

This girl asked her, "Why do you call that thing Seymore?"

" 'Cause he can see you. Seymore's always watching you." She winked.

Ms. Valdez can get away with being such a freak because we're at an "urban" high school. "Urban"'s code for "ghetto" and Willmore can be pretty dang ghetto if I don't say so myself. Like, we're the most ethnically diverse high school in America which pretty much means that there aren't a lot of white people here and things get a little tense with gangs and with stupid Mexicans calling Blacks "mayates"[8] and angry Black kids telling Mexican kids to go stand on the freeway and sell oranges, and everyone calling Asians "nips" when that's really a Japanese slur and the people getting called it are probably Hmong, Cambo, Laotian, or Thai.

I've figured out that the way things work around here is that as long as a teacher can control us and there aren't total race riots happening everyday, administrators look the other way when it comes to eccentricity. Ms. Valdez might wear tight black dresses with flaming skulls on them and fishnet stockings and necklaces with rhinestone spiders but everyone's down with it cause she's got us in check. Now, if she were to go teach in, say, Orange County, she'd have to chew with her mouth closed, buy a whole new wardrobe, and quit with the longshoreman talk.

I looked around. A fan stirred hot air and Ms. Valdez's room wasn't as full as it usually is at lunch. By the rear bookshelves, this boy who I think is autistic was playing an Asian guy at chess. Three light-skinned Black girls were huddled around a yearbook, whispering. This Filipino glam rocker, Damien, was sharing earphones with his best friend, this cute Black girl with clear braces, Portia. They looked borg-like, their heads connected by white wires, bobbing to the same beat.

"Hey," I said to Damien. He popped out his earphone and looked up. Portia took out hers, too. I stared at Damien. He wore blue eyeliner that started at the tip of his eyebrow and descended halfway down the bridge of his nose. "Wassup with the makeup?"

"That's my unicorn stripe," he lisped.

Real diplomatically, I asked a question I've been wanting to ask

---

8   Spanish equivalent of the 'n' word

for a while: "Are you a transsexual?"

He shook his head. "No. Just androgynous."

A black boy wearing a do-rag popped his head in the door. He said, "Gimme two dollar, nigga," to Portia.

"I ain't no nigga!" she yelled back.

"Okay. Gimme two dollars, niggette."

"Fuck you!"

"Ay!" Ms. Valdez screamed. "Knock it off!"

"You ain't goin' gimme no money?" do-rag asked.

"No."

"Forget you then!" The boy left.

"Who was that?" I asked Portia.

"My sister's friend. He's dumb."

"I wanna ask you guys something," I said to Damien and Portia, "but first I have to talk to Ms. Valdez."

They nodded and popped their earphones back in. I turned and timidly walked over to Ms. Valdez's desk.

"Ms. V," I said.

She looked up and smiled. "Yes, Roberto?"

"Don't call me that!" I groaned. "You know I hate being called that!"

"That's your name, isn't it?"

"Yeah. But you know I go by Cassidy."

"Okay, Ca-ssi-dy. How'd you get that name anyways?"

"*The Partridge Family*. Re-runs of it. My mom liked David Cassidy."

"Poor you." She took her gum out of her mouth and stuck it behind her ear. She grabbed a red apple and bit it and chewed and asked, "What can I do you for?"

"You know the junior thesis that was due last week?"

Ms. Valdez took another bite and got lipstick all over the white of her apple. "Mm-hmm. The one you didn't turn in?" she answered, her mouth full.

"Yeah. I've got it right here." I pulled it out of my backpack.

"I don't know, Cassidy. That shit's a week late."

"But I brought you this tasty flan!" I blurted and placed it on her desk by a dry sea urchin.

Ms. Valdez busted out with Santa Claus laughter. "Kid, you sound like Napoleon Dynamite going, 'I caught you this delicious bass.' Kudos to you, Cassidy! Just for having the balls to bribe me, I'm gonna accept it one week late and I'm only gonna dock ya ten points. The maximum grade you can get on this is ninety out of a hundred."

"Can you grade it for me right now?"

"Don't push your luck."

"That's cool, that's cool," I said, backing away.

I started to turn around, but Ms. Valdez said, "By the way, what'd you do your thesis on after all?"

I grinned. "*Catch-22*."

"Yeeeees," she coaxed.

"I argued that Yossarian's a homo."

"How'd you support that supposition?"

"Easy! The first line in the book is about him falling in love with a dude. Love at first sight, man!"

"Fair enough. I'll let you know by Friday what your grade is."

"I did the math. This'll bring my grade up to 60%, won't it? Even if I fail the thesis?"

"Yeah. This," she touched my paper, "will ensure you pass. Hell, it might even bring you up to a C if it's any good."

"Awesome. Okay, see you later, Ms. Valdez."

The bell rang.

"See ya, Cassidy."

I walked back to the borg. "Hey," I said. "So, the question. Did you guys do your history homework?"

"The worksheet on Chapter 25?" they asked.

"Uh-huh."

"No."

"Damn. I was going to ask if I could copy it."

Damien and Portia unplugged their earphones, grabbed their bags, rose and the three of us left Ms. Valdez's together, dragging ourselves north, across campus, to fifth period, US History. It's right upstairs from Mrs. Kiku's and we hate that class. Everyone hates it because the teacher, Walker, is an uptight little bitch. He thinks Bush is God's gift to America and every Monday, we do what he calls "Update: Iraqi Freedom." Walker leans against the podium and tallies how many people we've killed over the last six days in the Middle East while he guzzles black coffee. All the excess caffeine makes him paranoid and he wears Chester the Molester glasses and Lee jeans and hiking boots and he suffers from Napoleon Syndrome—he's barely five one. Dude spends way too much time hanging out with Hispanic female students during tutorial and his version of US History is an embarrassment. When we did Vietnam, he skimmed over the anti-war movement and only devoted one sentence—*one sentence*—to Nixon's invasion of Cambodia.

I know about the mess that happened over there cause I like reading about war and stuff. Sokhun told me gory details about the Khmer Rouge and my mom's sister, my punk rock Tia[9] Shelley, has the Dead Kennedys' single "Holiday in Cambodia" in her vinyl collection. When I listened to it, I heard Pol Pot's name for the first time and Sokhun told me about how he was a communist dictator who created his own time cycle starting at year zero and he set up these re-education camps which were basically the Cambodian version of the Holocaust where you got sent to work or die. Sokhun's mom and dad almost went to one cause they wouldn't stop being Buddhists and Sokhun's dad

---

9   Aunt

wears glasses. According to Pol Pot, glasses were a sign of subversion.

Her parents escaped to a refugee camp in Thailand where her oldest sister was born and then they came over here like a lot of Cambodians did. Sokhun told me that Long Beach has the highest Cambodian population outside Cambodia and it's obvious driving down Anaheim Street. All you see is Cambodian shops and restaurants, pho noodles and straw flip-flops. It's Little Phnom Penh.

Me, Portia, and Damien waited in the hallway, trying to kill time before we had to go into Walker's and Portia saw her twin, Alexis, pass by. "What we doin' today in history?" she asked her.

"Watchin' a video."

" 'Bout what?"

"Ronald Reagan."

"Ugh!" Damien wretched.

The bell was thirty seconds shy of ringing so the three of us walked into class and took our seats.

"Get out your homework and pass it up," Walker said.

The bell rang and Walker walked from the left side of the room to the right, collecting papers from the first person in each row. When he was done, he counted. He made a pissy face. Only five people did his worksheet. He shook his head with disgust and carried the little pile to the inbox on his desk and set it on top. Then he turned and walked to the podium and straddled a little shelf on the bottom of it with one foot. Walker leaned against the stand and gripped the sides and said, "Today we're watching a video about one of our most charismatic leaders, the fortieth president, and one of my personal heroes, Ronald Reagan. Hopefully, as you watch, you'll understand why he ranks right up there with Ike and Bush."

Somebody chirped, "Kennedy!" in a helium sucking voice. Walker was not amused. Same voice chirped, "Clinton!"

Walker folded his arms and his mouth settled into an angry line.

"Thanks to your classmates' immature behavior. We'll all be staying one minute extra after the bell."

Portia whispered, "Fuckin' Rasheem!" and reached around and shoved the boy sitting behind her. He just giggled.

Walker turned out the lights and hit play and I put my head down. The VCR, our babysitter, was going to sing us a lullaby. The last thing I heard before conking out was, "...one for the Gipper!"

Portia was shaking my arm. Drool coated it and left a snail trail across my desk.

"Cassidy, c'mon! Your girlfriend's waitin' outside!"

Sokhun! My eyes opened. My head shot up.

"Oh! Shit!"

I wiped my mouth, fixed my glasses, grabbed my backpack and jammed outside. I saw Sokhun from the back first, standing by the drinking fountain. She was wearing her white Vans with the pink skulls, jeans, and a blue shirt. She had her Roxy bag slung over her shoulder. She turned around. Her face was pink, like strawberry ice cream, like the skulls on her shoes. Too much crying.

"What's wrong?" I asked. "Did your mom and dad find out your sister's gay?"

She shook her head and her soft hair brushed her shoulders.

I started to get seriously worried. "What's wrong then?"

She shook her head again. She folded her arms. "We can't talk about it here."

"Okay. Let's go then."

We both started walking. I had no idea where we were going, but we turned the corner by the girls' bathroom and walked down the stairs at the end of the hall and headed out the exit beside the cafeteria. We crossed the lawn, cut through the pines, passing the auditorium. We crossed the street and walked past the 98¢-and-Up store and stopped at the corner. Delightful Donut loomed behind us. I could smell the dough boiling in the grease. We still hadn't said a word.

"Sokhun. What's wrong?"

She started to cry.

"Please? You're scaring me."

"Can we sit down?"

"Okay." I started walking towards an empty pink table.

"No! Let's go behind."

We walked around back together. Sokhun squatted next to a dumpster. It smelled sweet and rotten from the donuts in the trash. Sokhun was creeping me out. I knew she was going to tell me something I didn't want to hear, something no guy wants to hear.

"I'm pregnant."

There. That was the big secret. I knew it from the minute I heard her voicemail but ignored it like maybe if I didn't think about it, it'd go away. But here was the proof, her confession swirling in the air. I had to face it. I couldn't pussy out. I had to be a man about things, even if my example wasn't the best. My dad, Roberto, left when I was three. My mom told him to pick us or meth and he picked meth. That's a tweaker for you.

I want to be a better man than him. I reached for Sokhun's hand.

"Sokhun, it's your body. You have the right to choose what you wanna do. I'll support you. I'll do whatever you want me to."

"Good. Because I already know what I wanna do."

"What?" I expected her to say, "I want to get an abortion."

She said, "I'm going to induce a miscarriage."

"You mean get an abortion?"

"No. I mean we're going to do this ourselves."

I felt sick. "How?"

"I've already started. I've been drinking this tea since yesterday. It's

38

made of tansy. It's supposed to make me have my period and miscarry. I'm already getting weird cramps."

"What's it made of? Where'd you get it?"

"It's tansy tea. Tansy's just a flower. I got it at an alternative medicine store on 4th Street."

"How do you know about it? How do you know it's safe?"

"I looked up how to induce a miscarriage online and there are all these sites with information on herbal abortions. Tansy's the strongest of all the herbs I read about. That's why I picked it. I need something that's not gonna let me down."

"How does it work? Will you just like, have your period and then, everything comes out?"

She shook her head. "You have to help me."

I gulped. "How?"

"Well, first we have to loosen my cervix. Get it to relax and open up. So we need to have sex. Or, I at least need to have an orgasm."

"Alright."

"And, we need to make my body freak out and want to get rid of it. The tansy should do most of the work but one of the websites I was on said that causing trauma will definitely help things. You're gonna have to kick me."

"Kick you!"

"Yeah."

"Sokhun, I can't kick you. This is crazy. Why don't you just go to a doctor and get a normal abortion? I'll take you. I'll help pay for it."

"I can't!"

"Why not?"

"Because my parents will kill me if they find out!"

"How're they going to find out?"

"I don't know! Like, parental consent or some shit like that! They'll find out! They'll throw me out. They think abortion's murder!"

"Buddhists think abortion's murder?"

She nodded. "Cassidy, I don't wanna talk about this anymore. I'm not feeling good. Can we please just go to my house and get this over with?"

I nodded.

We got up and walked around to the front of Delightful Donut to wait for the bus. It came quick and we boarded the 32 and transferred to the 41. We got off at Alacran and Cage and walked in silence to Sokhun's yellow house. Because Sokhun's parents are always working at her uncle's store, we get the place to ourselves a lot. That's where we do it; we have sex on her creaky twin bed with the purple Ikea comforter. When we first started doing it, we used condoms Sokhun stole from the pharmacy section of her uncle's shop. That pack ran out quick. She never got more.

Sokhun unlocked the front door. We entered the empty house and turned down the hall and walked into her room. She's the only kid still living there. One of her sisters is in college and the other one's a lesbian who lives with a girlfriend she passes off as her roommate. Sokhun sat on her bed. The stuffed animals on her shelf stared at me. The white desk with books arranged on it looked like it belonged to a smart girl. A poster of The Strokes hung on the wall next to a postcard from Angkor Wat. A serious, regal Buddha observed from the corner.

"We have to have sex," Sokhun said.

"What if I get you pregnant again?"

"Then just finger me."

Sokhun unbuttoned her jeans and pulled them down. She lay down on her bed and I crawled beside her and curled into her body. I felt her flat stomach and stroked the hair between her legs and felt her sigh. I pushed a finger in and felt her clit. It was hard and warm. I stroked it and tapped it and pinched it and played with it and felt Sokhun getting tense under me. It was working. I rubbed harder and faster and she moaned and then I stuck another finger in her pussy and felt her spasm as she came.

My hand felt sticky. I opened my eyes and held my hand in front of my face. Blood coated my middle finger. Sokhun saw.

"It's working," she said.

She pulled her pants the rest of the way off so she was only half dressed and slid off the bed. She went to the corner and picked up a golf club.

"Cassidy," she said. "You're going to have to hit me as hard as you can across my pelvis with this."

I stared at the club. I thought about golf vocabulary. 6 iron. 7 iron. Driving iron. Mommy dated a caddy once.

"Whose is that?" I asked.

"My Dad's. Cassidy, did you hear me?"

"I can't hit you!" I screamed. "I love you! Please, can't we just do this the normal way?"

"No! And if you don't help me right here right now, I'll just shove something up myself and cut it out of me! Okay!"

I felt tears in my eyes and nodded.

Sokhun handed me the club and got back on the bed. I looked down at her skinny body and thought about the baby in her tummy. I held the club limply in my hands.

"Do it," she said.

I lifted it in the air and angled it towards the middle of her body. I shut my eyes and breathed. I thought of Mount Fuji, of drifting down the sides of it, of seeing the calm waters of Lake Kawaguchi. I raised the club and brought it down with all my might, more than I thought I had and when I opened my eyes, the only color I saw was bright, bright red.

White Girl

She took me in her arms and came at me with a knife. She was my first white girl. Pale skin, green eyes, and stringy black hair. She cut her name into my leg. She bit and licked and sucked at the wound. The gash in my leg made me vulnerable and open, a surrogate hole, a place for a tongue or a finger to trace.

It all started with her sister, Mickey. Mickey was my best friend and Gabriella was her older sister. Mickey was short like me with kinky curly hair, gaps between her teeth, freckles, and a body like a sack of bones. She was knobby-kneed, knobby-elbowed, with a long skinny neck like a chicken. She was a tomboy with a crush on Axl Rose.

I became her best friend. We both went to St. Bern's Catholic School and our lockers were right beside each other. I'd stay the night at Mickey's house all the time and she lived way out, far from the edges of town in the middle of a quiet valley. I loved going to her house. In the middle of the night, we'd sneak out and go walk down the desolate country roads, feeling our way in the dark, listening to the hooting of owls and shrieking of bats. We were country girls, lost and lonely, and we'd found each other. We'd be miles from her house and there was a tiny graveyard on the side of a hill and we'd sit there in the dark beneath the oaks and hold each other. Sometimes a warm California breeze would come and rustle the air and our hair would stand on end and we'd giggle, snuggling even closer, like two small sisters. We'd walk home holding hands, through her grandmother's pumpkin patch, and sneak in through the side door of the house.

We both turned goth at the same time. We both went and bought combat boots but I also got pointy-toed witch boots with buckles and we also shared Wet'n'Wild black lipstick. We bought records and put black lace up over the windows and played "Bela Lugosi's Dead" over and over until it drove our parents crazy. We painted our nails black and gave each other fucked-up haircuts. We were twins in everything for an entire summer. It was hot and dry and it was like our honeymoon. Somehow, Gabriella managed to change that. She was weirder than both of us and had a boyfriend. She wore this really severe black hat to school and slave bracelet me and Mickey were jealous of. Everybody was scared of her boyfriend Willy and they said he was creepy and liked to kill animals and look at the insides, but I liked Gabriella anyways. She found a rusty old Chevy pickup, like a '39, and fixed it up herself. She didn't customize it or anything, just reached in under the hood and found a way to stroke it, make it come to life, grease it up and make it hum again. It would rattle down the road, angry, burning oil, filling the air with a dirty smell.

Gabriella and Mickey taught themselves to skate and they'd throw their beat-up boards in the bed of the truck and ride into town to find smooth places to practice tricks. They'd pick me up and I'd go with them. I'd usually just sit on the curb and watch as they'd ollie over things, sliding down handrails and jumping trashcans. I'd just sit and watch and wait until it was time to go home again and we'd all pile back into the truck, cramped in the narrow front seat like sardines in a tin, and rattle home. Gabriella would come to my house and pick me up on Friday nights and take me to see Mickey. After Gabriella broke up with Willy, she started to hang out with me and Mickey more. Gabriella would pull up my parents' driveway in her big loud Chevy and I'd run out of the house, kissing my mom goodbye, leaving a big red lipstick stain on her gaunt cheek, and she'd call after me in Spanish, yelling at me to be careful, a strange look on her face, trying to figure out these strange white girls that had become my friends, pale as ghosts, Anglo phantoms.

I was kind of intimidated by Gabriella at first, but slowly, we became friends. She would sit and drive and smoke and eventually offer me a cigarette, a Camel or one of her cloves. Her eyes were so green and you never could quite make out the shape of her body because it always swam in oversized black t-shirts and baggy men's trousers. Every once in a while, she'd bend to shift or make a sharp turn and her clothes would mold themselves to her body and just for a second you could see the girl that was underneath all that, swaddled in black, wrapped in a masculine package, and I'd wonder what was line and what was curves. We'd have dreamy conversations all the way back to the farmhouse and then her and me and Mickey would listen to records and light candles in Mickey's room and watch *The Hunger* for the twenty-fifth time and Mickey's mother would walk in during the part where the two women are in bed, licking blood from each other's wounds and she'd drop Mickey's laundry on the floor and give us a weird questioning look and turn and leave. "My mom doesn't like us watching this movie," Mickey told me. "We only watch it when you're here."

My mother was horrified at what my room turned into during those years. It was more of a coffin than a room, and everything was dead and covered in layers of dust, dead dried roses filling cheap dime-store vases, Mexican shawls from the my mother's girlhood draped over every piece of furniture in my room, Victorian antiques brought here from Guadalajara, some of the only furniture willed to my bastard grandmothers becoming co-opted into the dark circus that was my little bedroom. I think that the worst for her were the Catholic icons, the Virgin, all the images and icons of the Virgin with a mournful look on her face that I gilded with black lace and barbed wire, my rosaries that we had blessed at la cathedral in Mexico, and the votive candles that burned alongside tattered copies of *Dracula* and *The Labyrinth of Solitude*.

Sometimes Mickey and Gabriella came over to my house but most of the time we were at theirs. I lived closer to town but we could get away with more stuff at their house because their parents weren't as strict. Sometimes they got pissed and made us stay home but most of the time it was like they just didn't care. They let their daughters run wild. The sisters didn't really like to come to my house. They didn't like my mom's food and Mickey always made fun of her 'cause she had an accent. They didn't get that part of me at all. Their parents were Catholic, too, but it was different. They thought my mom's things were stupid: lots of icons, big heavy ones; statues; colorful paintings with weird subjects; Indian things from Mexico. I suspect that deep down inside, because of her accent, they believed she was stupid and could be easily deceived. But she wasn't stupid and she saw right past everything, through them, through the dark clothes, the messy eyeliner, the dog collars, and their cold angry stares. She saw right into Gabriella's chest and into her heart and knew what made her heart beat and saw the girlish desire that lay there and they had underestimated her terribly.

The three of us shopped at the Catholic Charities Thrift Store, the one by the railroad tracks and this rowdy Mexican bar called El Gato Negro. We poured through the smelly racks, finding treasures to take home and repair. I was wearing June Cleaver dresses dyed black paired with my buckle boots and fingerless gloves. I wore very proper hats with mesh covering my hazel eyes and I ate very little, as little as I could. I wanted a small waist. I liked Gabriella a lot and she always went to the men's section to scour the shelves for old suits, three-piece ones, and she looked so awkward and beautiful at the same time. The three of us loved thrift stores, the smell of mothballs, used dead things, and each other. We were a trio with an unspoken romance and nobody every talked about how close we felt, like the three of us were connected by something tangible but somehow invisible, being fed by the same clear umbilical cord that made us all sisters.

That changed the day of the poems. I wanted to show Gabriella just how much I really liked her, what a cool girl I thought she was, that she didn't give a shit that all the nuns and the priests hated her, and that she was the number one rebel who'd stolen my heart. I sat in my room one night, listening to my Billie Holiday records and wrote all the words to "You're My Thrill" and then cut my arm and squeezed blood onto the tip of a needle. I wrote out the words of the song in my blood and I felt warm and safe and scared all at once. I had asked Gabriella to meet me in front of the school chapel the next morning 'cause I had something to give her.

She was sitting there, waiting for me at 7:30 and I slipped her the rolled-up piece of paper and my hands trembled. "Here," I told her. "I made this for you but don't open it until you get home."

"Why?"

"Just don't." I blushed and smiled and walked away.

I sat in every class, looking at the clock, wondering if she'd really wait, sprinting to Tony Montecinos' car when the bell rang. He was this mod boy who gave me a ride home from school everyday in his Volkswagen and he took me home and I waited. My stomach tied in knots and the phone never rang. I wondered what she'd think when she read it. I wondered if she'd hate me and I wondered if she'd be disgusted. I wondered if she just wouldn't care, and I think that was the scariest of all my thoughts. The next morning, I walked to Gabriella's locker and she stood there with a crooked smile on her face.

"Here," she said to me in the softest voice I'd ever heard her speak in. She handed me a small piece of paper folded into many pieces. "You can open it whenever you want."

I blushed and sat and opened it and she sat next to me. I could smell her. She smelled like shampoo and mildew. She had a small pimple by her lower lip. She wore a green shirt. I loved every single thing about her. I opened the paper and found a letter telling me how she felt about how I felt. She understood. Her heart was the same as mine and in the same place. We had found each other and inside we were holding hands.

That weekend we had something like a date. On Saturday afternoon, she drove up in her truck and picked me up. I dressed up for the occasion: a long, torn dress from the 1930s, so thin you could see right through it, with a black slip from Kmart beneath. Black stockings and Victorian boots with sharp little heels. Gloves and a black bolero jacket, embroidered. I had cut my hair in a sharp Louise Brooks A-line to go with the dress. I grabbed a black handbag and was ready for her. She stood at the door, waiting. She had dyed her hair black again and it looked brittle and dry. She stared at me with green eyes, two large almonds that peered out from behind sharp cheekbones, part gentleman, part lady. She wore a three-piece suit with a pocket watch and black shoes.

"The suit was my grandpa's," she told me. "So was the watch."

We walked to the car together and rattled down the country road as the California sun dimmed and dipped into the foothills. "This was given to my dad by my grandpa and then he gave it to me. My grandpa was only 23 when he died." She paused for a few moments. "I think I'll die young, too."

I nodded my head in agreement and smiled bashfully. We drove north in silence. My heart was buzzing inside my chest.

We stopped in a small town with the world's tackiest hotel—a huge gaudy pink thing that looked like it was made of ice cream—and went to a café with big metal flower sculptures jutting from the ground in its courtyard. Gabriella bought me a cappuccino and I sipped it really fast, trying to avoid the bitter taste. She bought me a second one and my pulse went racing and I felt drunk from the caffeine and from her smell. We walked through alleyways to the edge of downtown, enjoying the shadows, past a mission, and took the path that went under a bridge. We walked down to the water and stood on the rocks, listening to the sound of the water humming over the pebbles. There was no one around. She pushed me against the damp, mossy wall and stroked my short hair.

"You're pretty," Gabriella said softly. I thought she was going to kiss me on the mouth and I closed my eyes but instead of lips on mine I felt a warmth on my neck and her teeth were digging into me, biting, painful but sweet, and my thighs went warm. She bit at my neck for a while and my body went limp. I stared at the moon. She didn't touch me anywhere, just stayed like that, in that position, like a cat with a mouse, pinned to the wall, nowhere to run but enjoying every second of it, a soft little plaything. When Gabriella was finished, she stared at me, eyes twinkling, and I wondered what part of me she'd attack next.

We left after that, rode home in silence, and she dropped me off at my house. I tried to turn up the collar on my jacket to cover the bruises she had left but I'm sure my mother saw. She had left purple and red scratches, little echoes of her kisses on my neck, and I was proud of her mark. I went to my bedroom and took off my hat and gloves and dress. I stood there in my slip and plastic pearls, staring at myself in the mirror, running my fingers over the marks on my neck. I still felt warm and I loved my souvenirs. I took off my stockings and turned on my record player and turned off the lights. I crawled into bed and curled myself into the tiniest warmest ball and thought about her, the way she smelled, her skin, her black clothes, how her breasts shifted under her old vests and worn out t-shirts, what it feels to be close to a white girl, close enough to smell her clean scent.

Gabriella was exotic. She came from another world. Pale skin, green eyes, and casseroles for dinner. She spoke nothing but English. She was raised to fear the macabre and there was nothing dark about her except for what she invented and that made her powerful. It wasn't forced on her. I liked her for that and loved her for so much more.

My mom knew exactly what was going on. It was almost tangible, complete with an odor that came from my pores and filled my bedroom with girlish heat, puppy love and lust. I had met someone who made my insides feel like cookie dough and it was a girl. A girl who hated my mother's cooking because it wasn't bland enough and made fun of the way she killed English. Gabriella would be at the dinner table with me and my family and she'd slowly nudge her foot towards mine, stroking my little naked ankle with the toe of her big heavy boot. I'd feel warm and keep eating and she'd push food around her plate. My mom stared at us, able to see right past it all, two teenage girls playing footsie under the table, a foreplay she didn't understand and was scared of. I looked like I was on my way to a funeral, with my choppy black hair and my funny dresses. But I glowed. My mom hated the juxtaposition, the happy lightheartedness mixed with some sort of inappropriate, heavy passion and I had fallen so in love or at least I thought I had and I knew that I really wanted Gabriella to touch me anywhere.

There was so little to do in our town that we had to invent games to play and things to be a part of. Way out by the dry riverbed that borders town, there was a racetrack, the old Speedway, a California hick paradise where they served bad food and little kids with shit-stained diapers ran wild. The tomboy in Mickey was dying to go and Gabriella thought it would be fun. They eventually convinced me to go too, and we bought buckets of bright yellow popcorn and shitty nachos. We sat in the front row, the worst and most dangerous place to sit at the races. Grit and exhaust spat into our faces and our food and our cheeks stung from the tiny rocks that pelted us. The people there were scary. A few Mexicans, some people from the Indian reservation, drunk white men with big bellies, lots of babies, horrible sad looking wives. The husbands all wore those funny hats with the mesh in back and the foam fronts. They drank beer from cans and some younger guys shared their Coors with us and we sat there getting shit-faced and the guys wanted to get some, thought we'd be easy because we were three creepy girls. But they got pissed when we laughed at their suggestion.

"Fuckin' dykes," one of them muttered as we walked away, the three of us holding hands, giggling, dirty, and high.

We drove home, the long drive from one canyon to another, and finally arrived back at the sisters' farmhouse. Their house was so romantic to me because someone had died in it, an old man. Before they moved in, their mom had it exorcised. The priest went from room to room, sprinkling holy water and blessing the place. Nothing strange happened. Nothing moved or creaked or groaned but I liked thinking about the idea that maybe something was there in the house, something that had to be cast out. We pulled up and Gabriella parked her truck out by the barn and we all climbed out, still giddy and light-headed. We had run over a tarantula going up their driveway and its white guts were all over the dirt path.

We came in through the side door and Gabriella's dad was sitting in the kitchen with a glass of something and we all ignored him. He wasn't a very nice man. We went upstairs to Mickey's room and sat in the dark, talking. I took off my shoes and climbed into bed with Mickey, our feet touching, and held hands. I was so warm next to her. There was one dim light on and there was a record playing, I don't know what, something painful and whiny, and we stayed there and talked through midnight. One sister was on one side of me and the other on the other. Mickey had my hand in hers and she caressed it, her face buried into the pillow and I didn't understand what her caress meant but I enjoyed it. Gabriella sat next to the bed, her fingers playing on my cheekbones, tracing something back and forth, neither knowing if or where the other sister was touching me. I had both of them and I felt like the third sister. When Mickey's caresses stopped, I knew she was asleep. I wiggled myself out of her arms and from under her leg and grabbed Gabriella's hand. We slipped out of the room quietly, shutting the door behind us.

We walked across the hallway to her bedroom and closed the door as gently as we possible could. I put my arms around her neck; I had to reach up to do this, I was smaller than her, and I could feel her shaking. We were both shaking. Both of our bodies were taut, pulled tight with restrained excitement that was muted and dead and had nowhere to go. I could feel her nipples poking through her shirt. Her breasts seemed so full and she was totally and completely a girl to me in that moment. She continued trembling as I slowly reached down to pull off her shirt and she helped me, lifting her arms up like a little girl helping her mommy undress her for a bath. I dropped the black t-shirt on the floor and very slowly cupped both of her breasts in my hands. It was the first time I ever felt anybody's but my own. Mine were small, girlish and high. Gabriella's were real breasts like a woman's, like in a magazine, heavy and round, and I held them like they were delicate fruits. I thought that they were the softest things I had ever touched. I felt them slowly, like the priest lifting the host at the sacristy, ready to anoint and poised for the daily miracle of transubstantiation. I wanted them in my mouth. I touched my mouth to them and I felt a melting sensation, warm ice cream dripping down my chin on a hot summer day, cream and sugar, girlish things pretty and beautiful, white and warm. White warmth and white light. I touched them and she groaned and my mouth was so hot I didn't know where her heat began and mine ended but I continued to kiss and lick and suck and her nipples got firm and hard, ready to explode. My pussy was hot and warm and I was so scared I could not imagine being touched anywhere down there and I felt ashamed. I hated everything below my belly button and wanted to stay here, hungry forever, drinking imaginary milk.

Gabriella pulled away from me and I was so scared for a second that I'd done something wrong. When she took my hand and pulled me down to the floor, I knew I hadn't. I sat beside Gabriella on the bed and waited. There was a weird moment of awkward silence and I heard fumbling noises and then I saw her face and she was lighting a cigarette. She handed it to me and she switched on a night-light, an ugly thing in the shape of a clown's head, and she struggled to find something under her bed. She pulled out a box, old and beaten up and held together by duct tape. She folded her legs and took off the lid. I think it was a shoebox. I took a drag from her cigarette and gave it back to her. I stared at her in the dim light of the clown, big soft breasts, cigarettes, and a worn out shoebox. She pulled off the lid, reached into the box, and pulled out a knife that caught the dim glow, shining so faintly, the tip seemed almost delicate. She held the heavy thing in her hands, silently demonstrating its weight and its violence and in some mute way, how much she liked me back. The cigarette hung out of her mouth and she smiled.

"You want to," she asked.

I went weak. "Yeah."

Gabriella smiled bigger and it was a smile that I didn't understand but that I wanted to see again. She crawled toward me and wrapped her legs around me. She was still wearing wool pants. She pulled off my slip, stripping me to my old underwear, cotton panties that hadn't been replaced since I was 12. She embraced me and I didn't want to blink because I was so afraid I would miss something and it was all I could do to get myself to breathe. She touched the cold shaft to my thigh and it felt so cool and precise against my leg. She pressed my skin, going into my flesh, not cutting, just pressure, silver against brown and I waited. I put my hand on hers and wrapped it around her fingers so that we held the knife together.

"Let me," I said.

Gabriella let go of the knife and I held it in the same place for a minute or so, slowly dragging it up and down my thigh, doing it with a really light touch, not really doing any real damage. I pulled it up my leg again but on its way down I put pressure on shaft, broke the skin with it, the blade traveling horizontally down the length of my leg for her, to show her how ready I was for her, so she could see some part of me that was on the inside. Blood began to appear. At first, it was just a thin red line but then fat drops of blood began oozing out of my thigh and it felt so hot, everything centered in that one spot that we both stared at, my leg, and she slowly bent over, crawling around me, and I went backwards, propping myself on my elbows, watching her face, trying to read whatever I could from her blank expression. It was sexy, not knowing what she was thinking. She put her finger on it, the cut, and then fingered it gently, getting her fingers wet with the thick drops and running her index back and forth across the line, smearing me with it. I smiled the smallest smile I would allow myself. She reached over and put her mouth to it and I could feel her tongue in it, stinging me, really enjoying it and feeling for the first time another person making me tingle down there with a satisfaction that I would later learn to get with fingers and tongues and fists and cocks. But first, it was in my thigh, my wound, my open gash. My pussy came and my panties were wet and neither of us understood what was going on. My body tightened and then released with hardly a shudder and my underwear was moist. There was no violence in my coming, I muted it, softened it, becoming not myself at all. Gabriella climbed on top of me and held me and we fell asleep that way, not saying anything, but thinking about strange things and wanting more.

Primera Comunión

Before I was born, my abuelita had dreams about me. On the eighth month I was inside my mom, my abuelita started to pray. She would make my mom kneel with her, in the living room, in front of an icon of La Virgen. They lit candles and recited the rosary together, every day until I was born. See my abuela, my grandma, had a dream about me that scared her. She dreamt that she and my mom were in the house, and I was outside—I wanted them to let me inside. The Medicaid doctor told them that I was gonna be born a girl, but my abuela swears she saw me in the dream as a boy, a pale boy with big, blue eyes. I knocked on the door, but my abuela said that something wasn't right, she knew she couldn't let me into the house. I went around the house, looking through all the windows while my grandma held my mom, protecting her from me as I tried to crawl into the house. There was something wrong with me. My abuela went to the window to send me away, and she cursed me in her dream. I stared back at her, my tongue flicking in and out of my mouth como una serpiente[10], long and thin, split down the center, flicking, back and forth. That scared my grandma. She was scared I was a malcreada, born of evil—my mama needed to be cleansed. What else could it mean if I had the tongue of a serpent?

They were scared so in order to cheat destiny they gave me a name that they hoped would protect me. They called me Esperanza, "Hope." I seemed like a normal enough baby girl when I was first born. They told me I was chubby, with thick black hair, and when they pierced my ears after one week, they said I didn't even cry. My abuela hung big gold hoops from my years. That's how you tell babies apart in my barrio: the girls are pierced, with gold, stones, and gems hanging from their earlobes. Babies with jewelry. But my abuelita should have known she couldn't cheat destiny. She came here to escape from Mexico but found demons waiting for her in the United States, ones that are worse. They're in disguise.

Naming me Esperanza didn't help. What my abuelita didn't realize was that Christian names don't mean anything in the barrios of gringolandia. No, in my rumbo[11], you're nameless until your clicka[12] claims you and decides who you really are. Sure, we have birth certificates that might say Maria or Consuelo, or maybe a priest pours some water on your head and announces that as God's child you will be called Beatriz or Guadalupe. My abuelita might call after me on a Sunday afternoon, "Esperanza, ven a ayudarme con las tortillas[13]," and I might answer to the name, running to the kitchen to help her grind the corn with a heavy pestle.

But the truth is, until your homies gaze into your soul and see who you really are, your name doesn't mean anything. Your family, they want to change the real you, prevent the real you from ever happening,

10   like a snake
11   neighborhood
12   Chicano for clique
13   Hope, come help me with the tortillas.

and so the name they give you, it's an empty one. They'd rather not recognize the potential for evil as well as good that grows inside you, that from within your soul grins the smile of a sinner and criminal. But your clicka, they're not scared to see this 'cause when they look at you, they see themselves grinning right back. Your homies don't mourn the loss of innocence like your family does, your old lady remembering how proud she was the day of your first communion, tu primera comunión, as you got down on your hands and knees in front of a priest and took the host on your tongue for the first time. They know that, in the barrio, innocence is a lie and that the biggest lie of all is that you were ever really innocent at all. In the eyes of the world, you were born a sinner, a criminal, a whore, or a gang-banger. And with pride, your clicka gives birth to you and helps you fulfill this prophecy.

That's how I became Angel Malo, Evil Angel. The homeboys would pass me by while I was cutting class, kicking it in front of the store or at the park, waiting for trouble. They'd check me out and holler, "Eh, Espie, what are you doing, homegirl? Come roll with us." I'd take off with my homeboys and we'd get stoned, go cruising, and find trouble. The homeboys from my rumbo, Grape Street, they taught me all kinds of shit during those lazy days: how to steal, to cheat, and to fight. One day, we were cruising out around Southgate, and we were jackin' this truck. I was jimmying the door, and my homeboy burst out laughing.

"Look at her, check her out, dude. She looks like an angel with her smooth skin and big ol' brown eyes, a little boy angel."

I grinned at him, my homey Bandit, the one who taught me how to steal.

Then Lalo said, "Shit, she ain't no angel, and if she is, she's un angel malo, an evil, crazy-ass angel, in loco drag with a talent for crime."

We finished boosting the ride, and we took it to an underground body shop out in La Puente where it got stripped and sold for parts. After that, I became known as "Angel Malo" and, true to my name, I had it tattooed on my forearm: an angel with wings, standing on a green-eyed serpent.

There was this one heine, La Dreamer, who started to kick it with the homeboys, too, but it was different for her. Me, I was one of 'em, didn't matter that I had a pussy and tits. I didn't flaunt 'em and I might as well not even had 'em. But this heine, she was a straight up girl, a fine ass Grape Street girl with curves like a woman should have, and she wasn't afraid to show 'em. She never kicked it with the girls. It wasn't 'cause they didn't like her. There was just something different about her. Something macho about the way she looked at you and the way she breathed. Something different just kind of oozed out of her pores and filled the air around her. But no one really said anything about it 'cause she was so fine and they didn't mind having this heine around all the time. She was always fucked up and she'd give it up for any loco who'd kick down some speed, or even better, coke. Most days, though, she was just stoned with her eyelids fighting to stay open. She was a fine, pretty woman but her macho vibe also communicated something else, something broken, like she had learned too much about herself, like she was cracked inside. Sometimes, when the locos weren't watching, I could feel her look in my eyes and I could tell that she was thinking about things that the other locas in Grape Street didn't think about, like she wanted me to reach inside her and fix her. But I knew that until she showed me exactly where it was that she had been cracked, I could do nothing for La Dreamer.

The night that La Dreamer's father died, she showed herself to me. It was late at night and I was just kicking it, getting high, watching TV, *Sabado Gigante*[14], or some shit like that. I heard crazy banging on

14   the most watched Spanish-language variety show

the screen door and I went to open it up. Dreamer was standing there, all scared looking, kind of twisting her body, swaying back and forth. I knew from her scared look that something was wrong, but when I saw she was wearing a big ol' jacket, I knew something was really wrong. It was the middle of summer and she had on this big old parka. Something was all fucked up.

I opened the door for her to come inside. I was embarrassed 'cause it was so hot that all I had on was my boxers, a wife-beater, and tube socks. I had a new tattoo on my neck that was still healing and covered in Saran Wrap that needed to be taken off. I stood there, staring at her, waiting for her to tell me what was up.

"Angel Malo, can I stay here for tonight? You know I wouldn't ask if it wasn't real important. The jura[15] are looking for Chato and I gotta help him out. He did something for me that no one's gonna understand, especially not the pinche jura, so I need a place to crash."

She sat down on the couch and I sat down in my dad's old recliner. She put her hand in her jacket pocket and pulled out a cohete. The gun looked heavy in her hand, and she held it so tight, her knuckles were turning white. Chato was her brother. I knew by looking at her that he'd probably fired that gun and killed someone only a little while before she showed up with the weapon.

"Yeah," I said, "You can stay here."

"My dad's gone, Angel Malo. He ain't never comin' back. Chato blasted him. Chato found him, Papi forcing me to be Mami, and he went crazy. He blasted him straight away." She took off her jacket. She had blood on her shirt and arms. Her eyes looked empty.

I said, "Come with me to the bathroom, Dreamer. I'll help you get clean."

She followed me to the bathroom. She was silent as I helped her take off her shirt. She wouldn't look at me. I got a washcloth and

---

15   cops

washed the blood off her with warm, soapy water. Then I brought her a clean t-shirt from my room.

"Let's go to my room, Dreamer, my mom's gotta get up early to go to work and I don't wanna wake her up."

She followed me to my room and I shut my door. Dreamer sat on the mattress I had on the floor and looked around, taking in the small space that was mine. It could have been any homeboy's room: walls with pictures of girls naked or in little bikinis draped over the hoods of cars torn outta *Low Rider* magazine, tangled blankets on an old mattress, a black and white TV sitting on a nightstand, and a bong full of brown water in the corner. On the window ledge was a little statue of La Virgen that my abuelita gave me when I was eight years old.

I turned the TV back on and sat down on the mattress next to Dreamer. I let her lean her head into my lap and stroked her hair. Her muscles felt tight as I held her in my arms, and I wanted more than anything to fix her, to help her know that everything was gonna be okay. I wanted to exorcise the tension, the pain that was making her wound tight. I knew that drugs would help her to relax.

"Dreamer, I got some weed. Wanna smoke some?"

She nodded. I fumbled around with a pair of pants that were wrinkled up on the floor until I found a bag and grabbed my pipe out from the shoebox I keep it in. I fixed us up a bowl and we took turns hitting it, getting stoned until our eyes were like pools of hot liquid, our faces turning red with tired anticipation.

I leaned back and she leaned back, too, breathing real slow. Dreamer turned and looked at me and breathed on me, real soft. Then she said, "Thanks for letting me stay here. Thanks for helping me." She kissed me on the cheek and put her head on my shoulder. I kissed her back and felt her mouth open up and return my kiss. I could taste the flavor of smoke and resin on her tongue. She felt like wet velvet, and she looked like an Aztec princess from one of them velvet paintings they sell at the swap meet. I felt myself turning hot for her and I dug into her mouth and licked the insides with my tongue.

She started kissing me back harder, her teeth almost grinding into mine, moving on to chew my fat lower lip. She bit and tore at it until it felt like it was bleeding. It felt like my skin was turning to blood and mixing with her spit and skin and hair. I tugged at her long hair, curls dancing around her face and spilling around us as we went at each other's faces, wanting more.

I felt her legs open and she got on top of me, her knees hugging my hips as she looked down at me with a stoned look in her eyes. Excitement was welling up from within her tiredness. She took my wife beater in her hands and pulled it up over my head. She dropped it beside me. She rubbed her hands down my flat chest, twisting and flicking my nipples with her purple nails until they were rock hard. She dug her nails into my chest and took turns working each of my nipples until I began to buck against her, wanting her to stick something inside me, wanting her to fill me up.

"Do you wanna touch me, Dreamer? Do you wanna fuck?"

She turned my nipple as I said that and stared down at me. "Yeah, I wanna fuck you. I wanna taste you." She leaned over to kiss my cheeks, biting my neck and ears, dragging her tongue down my chest, licking to my belly button, stopping there. She slid down my body to pull off my shorts. She ran her fingers through the hair between my legs and looked at me down there. Then she put her face up to it and smelled. She put my legs over her shoulders and all I could see was her long hair and I felt her tongue press against me, starting to go back and forth. At first, she just kind of teased me with it, like she hadn't decided if she was going to eat me out. Then she shot into a rhythm and started using longer licks, working her tongue against my clit until it swelled like a dick about to come. She started to suck on it, like she was giving me a blowjob, and I bucked against her face, speeding up the whole thing. I wanted to come.

Dreamer sucked at my pussy and stuck in a finger. I felt her spit on me and then stick in more fingers. She had three inside me, pumping me with them as her tongue stayed on my clit, flicking it. I grabbed my pillow and put it over my face and yelled into it.

Keeping her hand inside me, I felt her face pull away. Her fingers were tapping away hard at my spot and I heard her say, "Do you want more?" Dreamer's voice was full of sinister hope.

I barely got, "Yes," as I heard her rummaging through her jacket on the floor. Slow, I felt something cold pressed to my pussy. She held it there, against my clit while she started to pump me with four fingers, hard and fast like she wanted to rip me open. I was so stoned I didn't realize at first it was the gun. I was so high and fucked into a state of coming that I didn't care what she fucked me with. I felt the cold shaft nudging in and out of me while her fingers moved to my clit, pulling at it, preparing me. The metal inside me was now screwing me like a dick and I felt my muscles close around it, like they wanted to pull the trigger. Dreamer had my life in both her hands and I wanted to give it to her, to be a martyr to her pleasure. My whole body shook and I thought I was gonna die.

I'm not sure how long I was like that, frozen, outside my body, but when I came back, Dreamer was on top of me, looking into my eyes. I saw the gun on the floor, covered in wet stuff, shiny and reflecting the light of the TV. Dreamer stared hard at me and I understood the look in her eyes. She looked like danger, wisdom, and tragedy. And I wanted to be with her. Her look said she was leaving the projects, leaving Jordan Downs and I wanted to fly with her. I wasn't afraid to follow her to some new and unknown place. I saw forests in her hazel eyes. She blinked and they became deserts. I leaned into her neck and whispered into her ear, "Yes."

Dahlia Season

(i)

Florecita Negra[16]

I used to pride myself on being a freak magnet. Yes, los weirdoes de este mundo[17] had a sweet tooth for me. Walking home from school, flashers would show me their nuts, and later on, during cartoons, I'd get up to go answer the knocks at the front door only to find a wet behind the ears Mormon missionary wiping his feet on our doormat. It was the '80s, and Nancy Reagan had taught me well. I knew to just say no because this kid was ready to get me hooked on drugs.

I think my Freak Magnet Hall of Fame moment had to have been the time that this fugitive who'd busted out of holding from the municipal courthouse picked my window to climb through. I was kneeling on my bedroom carpet, sniffing my Strawberry Shortcake doll's hair, its candy smell was like kiddie crack, and the male prisoner

16   Little Black Flower
17   the weirdoes of this world

crouched just a few feet away from me, looking really feline. He expertly lifted a long, thin finger to his mouth, maybe he was a thief or a pickpocket or something.

"Shhhhh," he breathed.

"Desiree!" the police chief out on our driveway screamed through a megaphone. He read from a prepared script, designed to calm me. "Don't be scared! He's only a plumber! He's only a plumber!"

Hah! I was only in second grade but not in the remedial class. Plumbers didn't wear orange jumpsuits with numbers stenciled on them. Not busted shackles on their wrists either. I looked the guy in the eye. I lifted my doll back up to my nose real deliberately and sniffed. The convict grinned wide: we were cool. He winked, rubbed his palms together, and dove beneath my canopy bed as a massive dragnet finished closing in around our house.

Since that moment, my pull's been tried and true; I am gifted with a strong flies-to-shit thing. Like does attract like and the loonies have a sixth sense that we're of the same ilk and all. To put it even more bluntly, if I were a scratch and sniff sticker, I'd smell like bananas because that's what I am. Totally bananas.

My parents made two major attempts to de-weirdoize me. One was putting me in Catholic School. The other was shipping me off to Mexico when I turned fifteen. See, what happened was, right before I started high school, my petals unfurled, and as it turned out, they were dark. I was a dahlia, an artist, a goth chick, what boys who dug females like me termed "death bunnies." It's funny, I work as an ESL teacher now, it's all about comfy shoes and loose pants, but at the height of my Elvira reign, I wore dog collars. Torn black fishnets. Mini-kilts. Christian Death t-shirts. Blood smeared across my mouth, my forearms sliced by ladies' Gillette razors. My scars, I'm a little ashamed to admit, my most prized accessories.

To Mom and Dad, a pair of uptight intellectuals, my undead caca was a painful disappointment. They were raised the Mexican way, with dignity, respect for your elders, and the Virgin Mary and godammit, they hadn't immigrated to California just so I could become a Yankee misfit. A little change of scenery, they figured, was what I needed to knock some Hispanic sense into me, knock the American nuts out. Mom and Dad especially wanted to give me a hiatus from the white girls—this pair of death rock sisters, Blaze and Malice—who I'd befriended freshman year. That spring, both bitches had convinced me it would be genius to spraypaint my walls, my bed frame, and my brand new blonde bedroom set shiny black acrylic.

So, summer before tenth grade, Mom and Dad drove me to LA International Airport. They waved bye from the terminal and I gulped, turned, and walked by myself down the gray-carpeted cuff, into the belly of an Aero-Azteca plane. Four hours later, the beast spat me out in Guadalajara, Jalisco, Mom's hometown and the city where she started her love affair with Dad.

To me, Guadalajara seemed like a ginormously scary Third World circus. When I'd visited before, when I was really little, I'd seen a kidnapping and a carjacking and lots of homeless kids with flies on their faces selling mangoes in the streets. Holding Mom's hand, this other time, I'd seen an Indian woman breastfeeding her baby on the steps of a cathedral get kicked by a policeman who yelled, "Guarda tu pinche pecho, cabrona[18]!" On my way to the airport the very last time I'd visited, I'd watched a fire eater's face blow up as he spat lighter fluid into a flame in the middle of a busy intersection. This poor lady, a midget with gigantic feet that made her look like a hobbit, ran out into traffic to cradle his burnt body. He probably died, but I'll never know for sure. My aunt just kept on driving. She was in a hurry to get us to the airport so we wouldn't miss our flight home.

Standing on the airport curb, waiting for the chauffeured VW

---

18   Put away your damn breast, bitch!

Mom had said was being sent to pick me up, I took a big whiff. The hot Guadalajara air had a raw familiarity. Its odor hadn't changed at all, a stink like a yummy smog and charbroiled meat combo I'd never confess to anyone I actually liked. To me, the smell was tasty the same way that spilt gasoline and permanent marker tips are.

I caught a whiff of something else and winced. It was myself. My own fear to be exact. Sweat soaking through the pits of my black wool dress. My black and white striped pirate tights stuck to my crotch, moisture sticking them to my toes. My right foot started to tap. Furiously.

I'd never stood on foreign soil alone before.

A clattering VW Bug pulled up in front of me, and a man with thick black hair and '70s-looking aviator shades hopped out.

"Desiree?"

I nodded.

"I am Adolfo." He ran around and opened the passenger side door for me. "I work for your Tia Fe[19]. I will be driving you to her house."

"Thanks." I started to climb into the passenger seat.

He waved both of his hands. "No, no, Desiree. You," he motioned at me, "sit in the back." He pointed at the seat. "I'm the chauffeur; you are the client. Please, sit here."

I grudgingly obliged as Adolfo loaded my bags under the hood, slammed it shut, and climbed back into the cockpit. He stepped on the gas, juicing up the jalopy, and he drove it out of the airport, out onto the bumpy beltway. We whizzed past cars and I cringed, shrinking, a thirsty daisy. I may not have been riding in anything as gross as a limo, but I still didn't like the being chauffeured effect. I wondered if the people in the cars around me could tell what I was, some kind of green-eyed American brat who didn't deserve to be shuttled around. I

19   Aunt Faith

glanced at Adolfo's reflection in the rearview mirror. He piloted the bug stone-faced, and his sunglasses and strong jaw made him look more like a virile terrorist or rapist than a lackey.

After about forty minutes, we arrived at the two-story house where Mom's baby sister, my Tia Fe, lived. Her middle class neighborhood had a funny English name, Mount Olympus Forest, and even though Tia's house really wasn't all that, it had a tall, Great Wall of China-looking gate surrounding it. The height protected her family, kept robbers and kidnappers out. Since Tia's hubby, my Tio Eusebio[20], was in the jewelry business, he and his brood were moving targets.

Adolfo opened the gate and pulled the car into the driveway. He came around and opened my door and walked me to the front door. He knocked.

"Aren't you excited?" he asked. "You have your three little cousins to visit here, and you've got your grandmother nearby and all your aunts and uncles, and maybe your aunt will take you to stay at the summerhouse by Lake Chapala. What a nice vacation!"

I nodded but an ugly hollowness gnawed at my ribcage and I could feel anxious waves swelling and tingling inside me. My chin jerked up, my eyes rolled back in my head, and my chest thrust out, both of my shoulders flinching, blades arching back violently. I knew my shakes probably looked like I was seizing, but I felt embarrassed relief afterwards, the same kind of feeling you get out of a rich sneeze.

From the corner of my eye, I looked at Adolfo. He was staring at me, but when he saw I was looking at him, too, he looked away. I hated when shit like that happened. People seeing my shakes was about as bad as them seeing my cooch not shaved.

---

20   Uncle John

Eeyore. Pooh's friend who's dogged by that stupid rain cloud. That's who I became my first two weeks in exile. That bitchy burro[21]. Except my rain cloud was tropical. Monsoonish.

Lying on my cousin's twin bed, my feet dangling over the edge, I thought to myself, "God, I wish my parents were British. If I were only Anglo-Saxon, my punishment would've been to send me to England. At least there I wouldn't feel like I was wilting." I lifted my arm to my forehead and held it there, like I was swooning.

By noon everyday, the Mexican heat melted me limp as the wicked witch being doused by water. My raccoon makeup ran, my dark hair frizzed and sweat droplets pooled in the creases between my calves and hamstrings. Guadalajara destroyed the nocturnal look I tried so hard to cultivate and the cockroaches that flew through Tia's house conspired with my loneliness to make me a miserable creature.

Watching Tia's help, especially her maid America, who was only like three years older than me, didn't help either. In Mexico, you don't have to be that rich to have servants, even plain old middle class people can have a brigade of them, and Tia Fe was no exception. I hated watching America, whom Tia called "mi niña[22]," slaving. She dusted, swept, and mopped tile floors all day and I couldn't bear the thought of adding to her load so I hid my clothes from America so she wouldn't have to wash them or dry them or iron them and I resigned myself to wearing dirty panties turned inside out, crust flaking off, down my legs and onto the ground for a good cause: I would not exploit teen labor.

Also compounding things, I had a bad case of the doubting disease, the Howard Hughes disease, the Saint Thomas syndrome: obsessive-compulsive disorder. It was undiagnosed so Tia and Tio just thought that it was vanity, shyness, or amoebic dysentery that kept me locked in their john up to two hours a day. In there, I was really performing these

---

21   donkey
22   my girl

esoteric rituals meant to ward off catastrophes only I had the power to prevent. I washed, checked, and counted, and if I wasn't doing my magic, I moped and dreamt about California, fantasized about being bitten by a vampire, reread my dog-eared, mold-spackled copy of *Dracula*.

I was on a slow part where Lucy was getting a transfusion to replenish some of the blood the Count had drained her of when a brainstorm swept through my gray matter. There was no reason for me to suffer any more undue sadness; I could orchestrate my own ghoulish fun here in Jalisco! I set my book facedown on the nightstand and went to find my cousins, Lourdes, Chata, and Diego. I discovered the three of them playing Nintendo in the master bedroom, and they screamed as I unplugged their game.

"Listen!" I told them. "Calm down. I have an idea."

I forced them to sit quietly on their parents' bed and listen to my short spiel about how cool it'd be to have a little adventure. We could have a séance to conjure dead relatives. Lourdes and Diego agreed that this sounded like a good idea. Of course, Chata, the middle child, remained dubious.

"Por qué[23]?" she asked, "Por qué?"

"Uh, to ask them questions about the future," I bullshitted. "Don't you want to know when you're going to get married and how old you're going to be when you die and how it'll happen?"

"No."

"Why not?"

She shrugged.

Ignoring her lack of enthusiasm, I shouted, "Come on!"

I led the way downstairs with Lourdes and Diego marching behind me, eager ducklings. Chata trudged, a dark skinned lamb to the slaughter.

Arriving in the dining room, I commanded, "Sit!"

---

23   How come?

I turned and began to pull the heavy drapes shut and heard chair legs scraping the floor. Shadow bathed the room, and I spun around. I could make out my trio of acolytes seated around the circular table, a big, empty armchair awaiting me.

I pulled out my Zippo, sparked it, and lit three white candles that were wedged into a candelabrum. I pushed the prop to the middle of the table and took my seat between Lourdes and Diego, clasping their hands in mine. I was officially a medium. My eyelids slowly descended and my head rolled back.

"Abuelitooooo[24]?" I beseeched in my best baritone. "Are you with us?"

My combat boot's steel toe thumped against the wood. The candelabrum leapt. Its three flames flickered like Gila Monsters' tongues.

Chata shrieked, "Aaaaaa!" Teardrops erupted and spilled down her plum cheeks. "Los muertos! Los muertos[25]!"

"Dammit!" I cursed to myself. I knew I shouldn't have trusted a middle child with an operation like this.

Tio came barreling in. He took one look at the scene and immediately knew what we were up to. Me and Lourdes glanced at him guiltily. His nostrils flared.

"Go to your rooms!" he yelled. "No more séances!" He turned to look me square in the eye. "And you... Don't even think about taking out that Ouija board your aunt saw in your suitcase! Oh...she saw it. And it's staying in there!"

To keep a closer eye on me, Fe took off work the last two weeks of my stay. "At last," I thought "I have someone mature to hang out with," and Tia did plenty of cultural things with me, like take me shopping at the mall, La Plaza Del Sol. She also took me to El Mercado de San

---

24   Grandpa?
25   The dead, the dead!

Juan de Dios, this labyrinthine marketplace where you could buy live chickens, voodoo dolls, and saddles, and later on, we went to the Museo Regional de Guadalajara, this dim museum where you could see dinosaur bones in one room and tools that monks used to self-flagellate in another.

One muggy afternoon, Tia led me on a tour of the crumbling, colonial part of town where she and Mom had lived as little girls.

"Can we stop here?" I asked Tia outside of a Catholic articles shop.

"Of course."

We went inside and browsed and I bought a black rosary and a crucifix.

"Let's take them to the cathedral to have them blessed," Tia suggested as the salesgirl handed me my change.

"Okay."

We strolled two blocks down cobblestone paths to the Metropolitan Cathedral, ignoring all the vendors selling cheapie trinkets out front. Up the steps, through the doorway and into the cavernous sanctuary, I planted my feet on the white marble floor. Below it was dusty catacombs full of dead priests. I wanted to rush down to them to see their coffins but then a flock of pilgrims caught my attention.

Shoot! I couldn't believe I'd forgotten about Inocencia. Santa Inocencia. Saint Innocence, the little Roman girl-martyr whose own dad had set her up to be killed for having turned Christian. He'd buried her, but in spite of having spent centuries underground, her body took its sweet time rotting. In Italy, zealots unearthed her pretty corpse and had it shipped to monks in Spain and somehow, la santita[26] had most recently come to rest on a silk bed only a few yards away.

Mom had brought me to see her before and now I was ready to become one of the looky-loos wanting to ogle and cluster around her

_____
26   the little saint

glass coffin. Leaving Tia's side, I approached the west wall where she slept. Ascending two small steps, I got as close as I could to the saint and then realized my nose was pressed to the glass. My hot breath fogged up the pane, and I watched the dead girl sleep, flaking, like snow. Snow White. Blanca Nieves.

Inocencia's skull had been sculpted over with wax and painted over to make her look like she was still made out of flesh, and I remembered the gallery of stars—David Hasselhoff, Charlie Chaplin, Elton John—that I'd seen at the Hollywood Wax Museum one Christmas vacation. She might've been kind of falling apart, but Inocencia was better than them. Her long white dress and crown of fake flowers made it seem like she was going to wake up any second and go stand in line for her first communion. I glanced at her gloved hands.

Mesh.

Through it, fingers.

Gray ones. Or really, just phalanges. Fleshless phalanges. I could see them through the holes. In a most advanced stage of human decomposition.

I held my breath. Finally, I let it all out.

"Ahhhhhh..."

"Bring out the Gimp."

Nito was a wan second cousin I met for the first time three days before flying home. He came to Tia's for dinner with his twin sister, Raquel, his mom, Patricia, and his dad, Eusebio's brother, Manuel. America held the door open for the family to enter into the foyer, but instead of following his kin past the Spanish-style fountain and into the living room, Nito mucked left, towards a tiny bathroom that only had a toilet, no shower.

Now Tia had made sure to forewarn me about his limp but I hadn't thought it'd be that obvious. In the kitchen, earlier in the afternoon, she'd diced something that wobbled and looked like rawhide as she'd explained. "Poor boy. Polio struck him when he was very little. What a shame. Desiree, try not to stare. It makes Nito very self-conscious."

I waited for Nito to emerge from the bathroom and watched him gently flick off the light switch on his way out. His left leg seemed

75

a good two inches shorter than his right, and I imagined that if his legs had hearts and minds of their own, the left one had definitely considered sabotage, harboring jealous and malicious wishes towards its more robust neighbor.

The painter Frida Kahlo had suffered from jacked up legs. So had the crusader who'd fixed our Depression, FDR. They'd still managed greatness, and like both of them, Nito wasn't just handicapped; he'd been born ugly, too. His face was long, a cross between a baboon's and a horse's, and the sum of his misfortunes had made him a classically introverted rebel.

"Ay, ese Nito," Tia had lamented back in the kitchen, "ese niño es 'un hippie[27].' "

To Tia, hippiedom spelled danger, but by my sophisticated American standards, Nito only rated as a garden-variety teen malcontent. I watched him hobble to the living room where he sat on the couch beside his twin, his chin-length brown hair tied into a ponytail, his Pink Floyd t-shirt and faded Levi's an inconspicuous uniform as far as I was concerned.

Eye-catching pink mohawk, now that spelled bad boy to me. So did safety pins jammed through a cheek or lip. No, Nito bore none of the outward signs of freakdom's subcultural solidarity I was used to reading for. But, gosh. That leg. I wanted to see it. Stare at it. Maybe stroke it if he'd let me. I wanted to give Nito the third degree about what it'd been like for his own limb to turn against him and stay small while the rest of him kept on expanding. I wanted to know if he'd screamed, "Grow! Grow, you piece of shit!" because in a tiny way, I related to his dilemma. Nito had no control over his extremity like I couldn't control myself sometimes. My thoughts ran in speedy circles, like starved hounds at the racetrack, and my body had its own agenda, too. I shook and sniffed and dug at my scalp and couldn't stop touching my hair.

---

27   Oh, that Nito. That boy is a hippie.

While I sometimes wondered what possessed me to do these things, I usually hid them pretty well. Nito, however, wore his shortcomings for everyone to see.

At three, for the afternoon meal, we all sat down to eat at the same table where I'd held my séance. Throughout the three courses, I tried getting Nito to lock his gaze with mine. He kept nervously looking down at his bowl of pozole[28] each time he noticed me boring holes through him with my eyes. The kid must not have been used to girls trying to get his attention, much less Halloween cuties like me.

As America cleared dishes and Tia served coffee and cake, Tio stood and raised his wine goblet. "Tomorrow," he announced, "we are going to the summerhouse, La Casa de Mama Fe[29]!" He nodded at his brother. "You are joining us for dinner. We will say goodbye to the summer and welcome autumn! Cheers! And good health to everyone!"

The grown-ups toasted, clink-clink, but I tapped my glass and smiled inwardly. The gods were blessing me with another opportunity to get Nito.

---

28   A traditional Mexican stew consisting of broth, hominy grits, and pork
29   The House of Mother Faith

A House of Incest

La Casa de Mama Fe sat near the banks of Chapala, a lake that'd sustained a Huichol fishing village before it was invaded by American retirees. This battalion of old white farts had pushed the Indians away from their life-giving water in order to set up an English-speaking enclave for wintering in, sunbathing in, and dropping dead at.

Tia's house was small compared with these ex-pats', but what it lacked in size it totally made up for in panache. Her hacienda glowed the color of pistachio ice cream, craggy arches and rock columns supporting its eaves. Neon birds of paradise flanked its front walk while Nelson, the old gardener who always wore the same cowboy hat, tended the loquats by the plaque with the estate's name chiseled into it.

I'd ridden to Chapala in Tia's car and the Lincoln came to a standstill in the middle of La Casa's circular driveway. Across the street, this generic retired couple was out for their afternoon stroll, and I spied on them from the rear window. The husband was very anthropomorphic, a steamed lobster shuffling upright in a polo shirt and khaki shorts, tube socks pulled all the way up his shins, big ol' feet stuffed into spotless tennies. The wife, she resembled a fine leather handbag, and she wore Jackie O. sunglasses with a purplish tint, a silky top, pedal pushers and Roman sandals.

In my head, I mused, "That's Bob and Karen. They're from Saskatchewan. Bob owns a chain of very successful luggage stores. Karen was a homemaker till that little macrame business of hers really skyrocketed! Who would've thought a hobby could rake in so much dough! They've got two kids, the doctor, a podiatrist really, and a pro-figure skater, Tawny—"

The back door opened.

"Desiree," Tia interrupted.

I spun around.

"Come and get your things. You're sharing a room with Lourdes."

I cracked my knuckles and toes and climbed out of the car and went to pluck my duffel out of the trunk. With it slung over my shoulder, I meandered up the front walk, "Bob" and "Karen" still on my brain as I walked through the house's wide doorway.

Where were they headed? To the water? I didn't get why people made such a big deal about it, about el lago famoso[30]. The summer I'd been eight, Dad had taken me to see it, and we'd ridden a glass bottom boat that was supposed to give us a view clear into Chapala's heart and soul. Slimy masses of green tendrils had slithered across the pane, teasing us. I'd pictured dead mermaids caught and strangled by the kelpy stuff, their faces blue, their fish tails doing a death loll.

"The growth is killing our lake," I remembered the captain explaining to me and Dad. "It's lowering the water level. Chapala will

---

30   the famous lake

drain like a leaky bathtub."

I turned right down La Casa's long, main hallway and headed towards my room. Decorative statues sat recessed into grottos and alcoves along the walls. The maid, Fermina, Nelson's wife, was tickling a fertility goddess lounging amongst lush plants with an orange feather duster. She had cranked the volume on a nearby TV high enough for her to listen to telenovelas[31] as she tended to La Casa's Precolumbian art. Engrossed, Fermina didn't see or hear me walking past her.

A swarm of startled moths batted wings inside me. I blushed and hurried into my room, dropped my shit on the floor, and kicked the door shut. I flopped onto the bed, hard. I looked at its twin, sitting parallel and pretty and made. Lourdes would be sleeping on it.

Last time I'd stayed at La Casa, I'd been twelve and slept in the exact same spot, but Fermina's telenovelas had gotten me busted. It started this day that I'd been putting on my suit, it'd been the sweetest afternoon for a swim, and standing at the foot of Lourdes' bed, I struck this pose like Samson, flexing my muscles.

"Chica[32]," I grunted, "who am I?" I curled my fist, bent my elbow, hardened my bicep.

Lourdes smiled, she caught on that I was pretending to be the Don Juan from the show Fermina had on full blast, and she morphed into my love interest from *Siempre Natalia*[33]. Like I'd seen on American soap operas, I reached for my lady and embraced her, tilting her head back, planting my closed mouth on hers. With our lips pressed firmly together, I pushed Lourdes back onto her bed and ground into her, mimicking what I'd seen male mammals—dogs, rabbits, coons—do to their bitches.

My fingers peeled down the top of Lourdes' bathing suit. I licked her chest, moving my tongue like a hungry puppy's. Two pairs of nipples

31   soap operas
32   Little girl
33   Forever Natalie

puckered.

Lourdes moaned, "I love you."

In my manliest voice, I answered, "Amor[34], me too."

We played *Siempre Natalia* as part of our daily swim routine till the afternoon that I had Lourdes down on my bed and was giving her a monster hickey and this shocked "Desiree!" jolted us out of our ecstasy.

Lourdes' racing heartbeat vibrated my taste buds. I unsuctioned my mouth from her flat chest and glanced over my shoulder.

Mom stood in the doorway. Her face was pale, her eyes absorbing the spectacle of my bathing suit dangling around my waist, Lourdes' chest glistening at her, all my wet spit winking as my cousin panted. Blood flooded all the capillaries in Mom's face and she turned candy apple red and the meanest blue vein bulged at her temple.

"Good little girls don't touch each other this way!" she seethed. "Get dressed and come outside and don't ever do that again!"

Embarrassed, we nodded and pulled away from each other and cleaned each other's spit off. We pulled our suits back on, and with leaden, though barefoot, steps, we trudged out into the hallway. Lesbian boot camp was kaput for the time being.

I sighed as I returned from the memory of that summer and then, I gave in to a sadistic urge to slap myself across the face. Satisfied with the sting I'd inflicted upon myself, I turned and fished Dracula out of my purse. I sprawled out comfortably across the bed and read and twirled my hair in peace till a flurry of excited voices carried into the room.

Nito's family and Eusebio's pregnant sister, Lupe, had arrived. I got up and scampered out of the room, down the hall, walking into a throng of people kissing and hugging below a giant Alpaca tapestry hanging in the living room.

---

34   Love

"Come! Come," Tia urged, grandly ushering everyone through the glass doors, out onto the patio to dine al fresco. She led us to her new equipal, this pigskin furniture you've got to own in order to qualify as a patriotic Mexican. With everyone seated, Tia and Fermina carried trays of food to the table. Eusebio laughed with his brother and poured shots of tequila with one hand, smoked a cigarette with the other.

Poolside, Nelson worked alone, straining for bugs and leaves with a long stick that had a small, netted bag attached to the end. God, I felt sorry for my aunt's helpers. They made me feel so weird. I looked down at my lap, at my hands, so I wouldn't have to see them.

After a few seconds, I tilted my head back up. I was sitting right across from Nito. I'd strategically positioned myself there so I could resume playing the same game I'd started back in the city. I looked into his eyes, trying to hypnotize him, trying to forget that my aunt and uncle basically had slaves.

"Look at me, look at me, look at me," I thought. The fucker kept looking away.

Lupe was sitting next to me, sipping 7-Up from a green bottle. Her husband, a clean-cut guy named German, placed a torta[35] in front of her. She glanced at it like she was going to barf. She unfolded a paper napkin and covered the thing up with it and then set down her bottle.

"Fe," Lupe said to Tia, "later on, we are thinking about going to the new nightclub, Club Ajijic. Maybe Lourdes and Desiree would like to come."

I glanced at my aunt.

"Would you like to go?" she asked me.

"Is Nito coming?" I asked.

Everyone's lips formed a surprised 'o.' Nito blushed. He wasn't getting out of this one so easy. His downcast eyes stared at his twice-bitten torta.

---

35   a Mexican sandwich

He nodded, "Si."

I cheered, "Goody! Then, I'll go, too."

I scarfed my sandwich down quick as Ms. Pacman, declared, "Excuse me!" and left the table, dashing back to my room. I slammed the door shut behind me, shed my clothes, and a series of kamikaze moves—a sprint across the newly waxed bedroom tile, a leap across the bathroom threshold, a grand jeté into the bathtub—landed me surprisingly upright below the showerhead.

I turned on the water and let the stream beat down on my head. I shampooed my hair, really massaging the soap in, stimulating all of my follicles, digging my nails into my scalp. I hummed to myself and rinsed and loofahed my body, starting at my widow's peak, ending at my ankles.

"The power of exfoliation," I thought, "should never be underestimated."

Eager to put on my face, I quickly conditioned my hair and shut off the water. I grabbed a green towel and wrapped myself in it and pranced back into the bedroom, trailing water behind me. I was ready to commence the beautification process.

Without giving a thought to electrocution, I plugged in my hairdryer and stood in front of the dresser mirror, brushing and straightening my shoulder length hair. I tossed my damp towel onto a chair and slipped into a perfect costume: black satin bra; a tight, black mesh top over it; maroon velvet pants; witch boots with enough buckles to drive airport security bat shit; and that new rosary I'd bought downtown.

The steam had evaporated from the bathroom, so I toted my makeup caboodle in there and set it on the counter. Opening its lid, my weapons became apparent.

Rice powder. Liquid eyeliner. Mascara. Purple lipstick.

I attacked my face till it looked like I was wearing a seductive mime mask.

Blot, blot, I kissed a piece of toilet paper and beheld my reflection.

Death. The DC Comics' interpretation of her. My current favorite heroine. For goth girls, the real superstar of the Sandman series.

I smiled. Death smiled back at me. Becoming her had been my goal. Mission accomplished.

I skipped out of the john with more razz in my step than any death rocker should have and hurled myself onto the bed.

Knock knock.

I heaved a big old annoyed sigh and got up to answer.

Lourdes. Her eyelids peeled back with wonder as she took in my outfit.

"That's what you are wearing tonight?"

I cocked an eyebrow, nodded.

"Ay!" she said and giggled.

I stepped aside and Lourdes plodded into the bathroom and went to shower. I settled back down on the bed and read Dracula and chewed my nails raw, consuming the little hanging tabs I made, sucking at my bloody fingertips. Bundled in a towel, Lourdes emerged to blow-dry her short hair that was cut into a toadstool shape. I snuck glances at her as she changed into her sedate clubbing outfit: a white headband, a flower print jumper, Buster Brown-looking Mary Janes.

She squatted down to buckle her shoes, and I thought of our soap opera summer.

"Lourdes—," I began.

"Si?"

"Never mind."

I madly twirled my hair and buried my face as deep as I could, trying to lose it in the final chapter of my book.

At dusk, Lourdes and I piled into Lupe's Pontiac, ready for Club

Ajijic.

We rode into town, through streets filled with dangerous potholes, circling around glorietas[36] with gazebos plunked in the centers and rose bushes tickling the edges. Lupe pulled up in front of the disco and bravely tossed a red-jacketed valet her keys.

"Andale, muchachitas[37]!" she commanded us.

Lupe got out and started waddling to the club's entrance and we skipped behind her. She held the door open, and I entered first, stepping into a dim interior decorated to look like the tropics. Green neon filament lit up nooks and crannies and corners, casting just enough light so that I could see that the plants meant to give the place a lush vibe were fakes.

Something winged caught my eye. I turned to look. A human-sized papier mâché toucan perched on a monster bird swing presided above the dance floor. I imagined it falling, hitting someone in the head, stunning them. After they regained consciousness, they'd be fine except for a life long speech impediment like a stutter or a lisp.

Buenoth diath.

Red and pink lasers flashed. I saw white faces. Blondes. Freckled shoulders. The girl with corkscrew curls was a redhead. Her body wasn't liposuctioned. Like some of the others. A pair of collagened lips. Americans. Canadians. Spoiled Mexican brats. I got it. I was at a bored, jet setters' hangout.

I followed Lupe to a table where German, Nito, and Raquel were already sitting. Raquel was smoking a long cigarette, like a Virginia Slim. She blew smoke out the side of her mouth, and as I plopped down beside, she looked at me like I was a pile of warm dog shit. I would've pitied her if she'd been nicer; she looked exactly like Nito, same long simian face. Her only redeeming attribute was her neck. It

---

36   roundabouts
37   Come on, little women!

had grace, was swan-like. I thought, "That bitch would make a great ballerina; that mug won't be noticeable from the cheap seats and being such a skeleton and all she could easily get tossed around by Prince Charming or whatever."

"My love," Lupe said to German, "will you bring me a coke?"

"I will!" I volunteered. I stuck my hand out. Lupe put money in it. I grabbed Lourdes, and we ran together to the bar. Leaning against its rattan counter, catching my breath, I asked her, "What should we get? For ourselves?"

"Screwdrivers!"

"Des-tor-nilla-dores?" I annunciated slow.

She nodded.

I faced the bartender and slapped down my bills. "Una Coca y dos destornilladores[38]!"

The guy fixed our drinks, slid them towards us, and made my change. We carried our glasses back to the table where everyone, including Lupe, had joined Raquel in a smoke. I remembered a TV public service announcement where a fetus floating in a uterus enjoyed a cigarette its mother was smoking.

Hah!

Lupe might as well have given the baby a drink, too. She was training it be a real swinger. I looked at Nito. He was tapping his cherry into an ashtray and pouting. His face looked so bitter it was lipless, and I turned, toasted Lourdes, and downed my screwdriver.

When her glass was empty, I mouthed, "Otra?"

She grinned.

Like ground squirrels, we darted back to the bar. "Dos desta-padores[39]!" I announced.

"Destornilladores?" the bartender corrected.

---

38   One Coke and two screwdrivers.
39   Bottle openers.

"Sí!"

We scored our second round, carried it back to the table and pounded, pretending our beverages were just macho-sized shots. My pulse raced, and I could feel my T-zone getting oily. The DJ spun David Bowie. I took the ditty "Let's Dance" as a sign. I turned to Nito.

"Want to dance?"

"I do not dance."

I jumped out of my seat and walked to his side. "Why not?" I asked into his ear.

"Because... I cannot."

I shrugged and grabbed Lourdes' arm and dragged her to the middle of the dance floor. Making sure Nito had a good view of us, I got freaky with her. I moved stripperish, gyrating, and I got an urge to twirl, so I opened my arms and spun myself dizzy. A couple of Duran Duran songs played, and then Jordy, the four-year-old French rap artist with the existential hit "It's Tough To Be A Baby" came on.

"Oh là là, bébé," I shrieked, hopping up and down, "C'est dur d'être bébé[40]!"

Me and Lourdes were the only ones ballsy enough to get jiggy to the little frog's song. Except for us, the dance floor was empty. To keep my courage up, I was going to need more vodka.

"Otra!" I screamed.

Lourdes nodded. We stumbled to the bar, and this time Lourdes slapped the counter. She slurred, "Dos destapatornilladores[41]!"

The drinks sloshed towards us and we scooped them up and stumbled back to our table. Sweat was soaking my bra and my crotch. I felt giddy. Lourdes' knees were buckling as she walked. She struggled to keep her head up. It rolled left, then right, then backward, then forward. She was a broke rag doll.

---

40   It's tough to be a baby!
41   gibberish

Lourdes fell on the floor trying to get into her chair, and Lupe yelped, "My God! How many have you two had?"

I raised my right hand. My pinky finger, my ring finger, and my flip-off fingers unfurled, poised in the air.

"This is your last one!" Lupe warned.

Raquel looked at me like I was warmer, wetter dog shit, but Nito finally seemed intrigued. Plopping down on my chair, I placed my glass in front of me. With my hands behind my back, I lapped at the booze with my tongue. I was a dog drinking from a tiny dish, a fat kid at a pie-eating contest.

Lupe yawned. "I am tired," she said. "I need to get to bed soon."

"You heard your aunt!" German said to all of us. "It's time to go!"

He and Lupe rose and headed for the doors and Raquel and Nito followed. Me and Lourdes staggered behind; walking like civilized Homo sapiens was too gymnastic a feat for us. We were the last to step out onto the sidewalk in front of the club. I felt the early morning coolness breath across my slimy skin. It gave me a yummy chill. I looked at Lourdes. She didn't seem cold at all. Inspired by Ajijic's toucan, she flapped her arms and hopped up and down.

"I can fly!" she screamed, "I can fly—"

I laughed and shoved her and she toppled, the Leaning Tower of Pisa leveled, *Ka-Boom!* Lourdes rolled on the concrete, giggling, and I straddled her, stuck my fingers in her gooey armpits, and tickled. Her giggling got hysterical and I felt her body writhing under me like an eel out of water and my face swooped down towards hers for a smooch and Lupe shouted, "Get off the ground this second!"

A strong hand yanked me off Lourdes and shoved me into the softly upholstered backseat of a sedan. In a daze, I turned to my left. Raquel. *Ew.* My head swiveled to the right. Nito. *Hubba-hubba.*

In English, channeling a dead Brooklynite's accent, I bellowed,

"Heya, Legs!"

My arm jumped into the air and landed on my cousin's knee.

Squeeze.

Gravity pushed my hand up his thigh. My palm made contact with something hard.

Nito's head eclipsed the front seat and his thin lips pressed to mine. An amateur tongue slithered into my mouth, advancing me from homo to hetero incest, and although the village of Chapala was encouraging the smashing of taboos, it wasn't helping me wreck the one I'd come to destroy. I'd wanted to infiltrate a crippled boy's pants, caress a deformed limb, feel up a gimp extremity, and Tiny Tim, he got to lick the insides of my cheeks and drizzle saliva all over my face while all I got was what? To cop an average Joe dick?

Veni? Vidi? Vici[42]? Not that night.

In La Casa's driveway, Nito peeled himself off me, and like magic, I wound up in my favorite pajamas, tucked safe as houses between clean sheets. At noon, along with sharp sunrays streaming in through the bedroom windows, a heavyweight hangover woke me up. I slowly rolled to my left to look at Lourdes. Her eyes were shut, but she was definitely awake. I could tell cause she was doing that wince you do when it's too painful to cry.

With remarkable sympathy for our conditions, Tia nursed us with trays of menudo[43] and Squirt in bed. She made sure me and Lourdes sipped our lime soft drinks till they were gone, but then Tio started screaming, "Fe! Feee! Feeeeeeeee!"

She left before she could watch us eat our entrees, and the second she walked out of the room, I looked down at my bowl and decided what I was going to do with it. I frowned disapprovingly at the hominy grits floating in orange broth, entrails steaming like they'd just been

---

42   I came? I saw? I conquered?
43   a stew similar to pozole but with tripe

ripped out of their animal owner, perhaps still capable of digestion. I would rather have eaten tentacles.

I eased myself out of bed, carried the disaster to the toilet, dumped it in and flushed. Why was it that the most unappetizing food known to the Mexican people was supposed to be the cure for la cruda[44]? It seemed like a menudo maker's conspiracy. Sorry Tom, Dick, and Jose, another animal's intestines weren't going to languish in mine.

Before ordering us to put on our shades, get our things and climb back into the Lincoln, Tia forced me and Lourdes to down three Tylenols and an Alka-Seltzer. We felt a little more human after the drugging and we said bye to La Casa and carried our stuff outside. On my way back past the birds of paradise, I wished for a cane. With one, I could spare my eyes and just shut them and let the tip of my baton do my seeing.

I slid into the backseat and Lourdes slid in beside me, and with her head on my shoulder, we shut our eyes and dreamt of absolutely nothing.

Somebody was grabbing my arm, shaking it. I opened my eyes. Chata. She looked excited.

"The phone was ringing!" she squealed. "I answered it. It's Nito! He wants to talk to you!"

I snapped wide-awake and grinned and Chata led me into the house by the elbow, to the kitchen, where the phone receiver rested on the counter beside the fridge. I picked it up, put it to my ear. Chata watched.

"Bueno[45]?"

"Desiree?"

"Si?"

"It's Nito."

44   a hangover
45   Hello

90

"Uh-huh."

"I want to see you before you leave."

"Tomorrow is my last day here."

"Then I'll see you tomorrow. I have to help my father in the workshop, but afterwards, I'll be there. At six o'clock."

"Okay."

"Goodbye, Desiree."

I hung up the phone.

"Nito is coming to see me tomorrow," I said to Chata.

She looked impressed and kind of dizzy.

"Wow," she said and it sounded funny, very, very Mexican.

At 5:55 the next night, Nito showed up on Fe's doorstep.

I opened the door and found him wearing a long-sleeved purple t-shirt hoodie, tight red jeans, and black and white soccer shoes, soft soled, not cleats. He had his hair fixed into a sleek ponytail. Nito wiped his feet on the doormat.

"Hola," he said.

"Buenas noches," I answered but what I was really thinking was that in America, Nito would've been jumped for going out looking like that. "Homo-faggot!" his attackers would've yelled right before slamming a fist into his nose. "How'd you get that limp? That gerbil you tried shoving up your ass say no and bite your leg?"

Gee. It was weird. I stared straight at the tight red pants. I guessed shit that came off as totally gay back home came off as crazy/sexy/cool here.

Without even being invited in, Nito began dragging himself from the front door to the living room couch. I followed and noticed how he was trying to disguise his limp as an interesting but self-elected gait. He sat on the nearest pink love seat and I sat beside him.

From an archway, Fe watched the whole courtship, looking

pleased as punch. Lico and me were keeping it in the family, not a bad Mexican tradition. Like royals, my people use incest to keep the wealth from spreading too thin. Fe turned and went to the kitchen and fast, she emerged with refreshments: a tray holding two lukewarm bottles of Squirt, glasses filled with ice cubes, a bottle opener. She set the tray down on the table in front of us and smiled.

"Disfruten[46]," she said.

We nodded.

"Bueno..." She folded her hands together and turned and left the room.

Nito popped the bottles open and poured soft drinks for the both of us and then after asking me basic logistical crap like how old I was and where my hometown was and what my favorite band was, he commenced to drone for an hour about music, drugs and philosophy. The pendulum of the grandfather clock in the corner swung, telling time, distracting me. My skin crawled to the ticking and I curled and uncurled my toes to the sound and when my feet got tired I shifted the movement to my butt cheeks, tightening and untightening them. Finally, I fixed my eyes on the pendulum, as if staring at it long enough, willing it not to move, would make it stop. Chimes began to strike seven.

"How old are you?" I blurted out.

"Twenty."

"Five years older than me."

"Can I have a sip of your Squirt?"

I grabbed my half-empty bottle and thrust it at him.

"I'm sorry," Nito apologized. "It's just, I get very thirsty."

"Here. Have the rest. Do you go to school?"

"No."

"I go to school. What do you do?"

---

46   Enjoy

"I work with my father. In the workshop."

"Jewelry?"

"Yes." Nito pulled a crumpled sheet and pencil stub out of his jeans' pocket. "I brought some paper so that we can exchange addresses. Here." He handed it to me. "Write yours and I'll write mine."

We took turns scribbling, and Nito tore off the scrap with his info, holding it out for me to take. I took it.

"I'll write you," he promised, "at least once a week." Nito swooped in, pushing his tongue down my throat, pulling away fast, panting. "I love you, Desiree," he said.

With the back of my hand I wiped spit off my mouth. "Uh-huh. Me, too," I mumbled.

Nito stood, his baboon face red and sheepish, and he limped out of the house.

Baby Che

My first month back home, I missed Mexico.

Like a bad, bad American, I romanticized my stay there, fetishizing the experience. On my bed, I sketched still lives of tropical fruits to the strains of mariachi records borrowed from my parents' music collection. I braided my thick hair and crisscrossed it over my head in imitation of Frida Kahlo. Just to spite the September heat, I attended the first day of school in a new wool beret I'd bought from the army surplus with my allowance money.

Returning home, I'd had a little epiphany. I'd witnessed the inequities of the Mexican class system with my own eyes, and, consequently, had palmed Dad's copy of *The Communist Manifesto*. Within hours of finishing it, I'd accepted its teachings as gospel. I knew, from the art hanging around our house, that the manifesto's guiding principles had led so many of my compatriots—Diego Rivera, surely a bunch of other artists—and I'd be no exception. A long tradition mandated that as a Chicana I go through a red phase. And so I did.

Yet deep in the throes of my one-girl cult, a cult that worshipped the warped memory of "My Summer Spent in Guadalajara," I never once stopped to consider how infatuation had me by the 'nads. I was so taken by my ethnic roots that I'd forgotten about my big mistake; I'd told a fucked-up Mexican kid I loved him. He believed me, and like Nito had promised, letters from him started showing up in my parents' mailbox. Hope, passion, and lust fueled his pen, and I tried my best to respond although my Spanish writing was only slightly above googoo gaga, leche, agua[47] level.

Damn, how the novelty of that correspondence wore off quick. What killed it? Let's see! Hours wasted erasing mistakes, perhaps? Paper cuts from flipping back and forth in a crisp English-Spanish dictionary, hunting for the right words? Anxiety about accidentally writing something super dumb, making a mistake like the honky ass priest who used to do Spanish mass on Friday nights at our church?

That fool had thought the Friday night gig would be easy; all he had to do was read his translated note cards, but one night, he preached to us, his congregation of immigrants and immigrant spawn, that Jesus became "embarazado" through his actions. The polite people in the pews snickered. The rest of us rollicked. Oh sure, the word sounded like "embarrassed," but it was a false cognate. "Embarazado" means "knocked the fuck up." Talk about a straight up milagro[48]. Screw the loaves and the fishes, the miracle at Cana, good ol' Lazarus rising from the dead. The white priest said Jesus was having a baby.

Blaze and Malice helped dampen my ardor for all things Mexican, too. Hanging out in my bedroom, going through my CD and tape collection, Blaze looked over at my record player and made a face.

---

47   milk, water
48   miracle

Vicente Fernandez, king of the rancheras[49], spun on my turntable.

"What's up with the wetback music?" Blaze asked.

I said nothing and everything, blushing, plucking the needle off the vinyl, sliding the LP back into its jacket, immediately rushing it back to my parents' "lame" record collection.

A week later, changing into our P.E. uniforms in the locker room, Malice asked me, "Desiree, what's up with the milkmaid hairdo?"

A jagged schism ripped through my heart, splitting it into halves. My coif didn't read neo-subversive. It read Swiss Miss, *Heidi, Girl of the Alps*.

I reached up to scratch my forehead. My hairline felt warm, bumpy.

My beret was giving me hives. I was allergic to revolutionary chic.

When I got home that afternoon, I retired the hat to the back of my closet, and once my rash healed, I seriously considered not saying adios[50] but buh-bye to the fantasy of "Mexico, mi tierra, mi patria... mi corazon[51]!"

As much as he loves Mexico, Dad talks a lot of crap about it. He once told me that during times of unrest, our people choose to follow larger than life leaders like they're rock stars when what they should really be doing is thinking about how to make political change last.

"Take, Miguel Hidalgo," he'd ranted and raved, "the supposed 'father' of the revolution. Or Morelos. Or the great Pancho Villa! Once the hero died, the whole movement they'd built up collapsed. Bam! Gone! It's sad. Nobody in Mexico trusts in systems. Only charisma. They'll sacrifice their lives for somebody's magic or personality, but put their trust in an institution with longevity," Dad turned smarmy as a

---

49   a song within a genre of traditional Mexican music, often focusing on love, patriotism or nature
50   bye
51   Mexico, my soil, my fatherland...my heart!

mafioso, "fuggetaboutit!"

Now I was learning Dad's lesson first hand. Without Inocencia's hands or Nito's leg as my Pole Stars, my one girl cult petered into nothing. I unraveled my braids and fixed my tresses back into a jagged 'do like Winona's in *Beetlejuice*. I sketched bats and hypodermic needles instead of bananas and papayas and melons. In the bathroom, my pink razors were unsheathed once again and bloody zebra stripes reappeared on my forearms. With ease, I again assumed the mantle of a Ministry-listening, Boris Karloff-watching, clove-smoking, all-American teenybopper.

Of course, I scratched corresponding with my pen pal off my to-do list. This didn't daunt him, though; Nito started phoning me. At first, his calls came once a week. That became twice, then thrice, then every other day. It made me feel sort of special that this guy who was practically on another continent always wanted to know what I was doing, but then again, it also bugged. Plus, by Turkey Day, Nito was dropping hints that he was planning on popping the big question.

I was only a sophomore.

The Sunday of our breakup, I sat cross-legged on my parents' bed, tracing the pattern on their pussy-colored comforter. Nito was moody because he'd called the night before but I hadn't been home. In my head, I pictured him wearing that same sour balls face I'd seen on him at Club Ajijic. I rolled my eyes.

"Where were you?" Nito demanded.

I sighed. I twirled the phone cord. "At a party."

"Where?"

It'd been held in a dirt lot by the dump, but I didn't know how to say "dump" in Spanish. "In an open space near where they put all the city garbage. I don't know what you call it. It stinks and it's dirty. It's full of trash. You know? All the city's trash goes there."

"El basurero municipal?"

That was it. "Si."

"What did you do there?"

I sucked my gums. "Hung out with my friends, Blaze and Malice. We watched two girls fight. Smoked out."

"Marijuana?"

"Mm-hmm."

"What a filthy place. And it sounds dangerous. Desiree, I believe you are smoking too much weed."

Immediately on the defensive, I argued, "Look, marijuana's all-natural. An herb. And don't lecture me about drugs. You told me that you wanted to go to the Lancadon Jungle in Oaxaca, get high and hallucinate with the Indians. See the face of God? Remember!"

"That's different! That's spiritual! You're my girlfriend and I don't want you out acting crazy. Smoking so much marijuana."

Nito's audacity incensed me. He was trying to levy an international embargo on my fun.

"You can't tell me what to do," I snapped. "I'm not your girlfriend."

"You have changed so much since returning to America," Nito whispered.

"That's right," I agreed. "I've got my gringa life here with my gringo friends. I think it's best if we stop talking. Oh, and I have a new boyfriend," I sort of lied.

"What's his name?"

"Alucard," I chuckled to myself. Dracula spelled backwards. I couldn't wait to tell Blaze and Malice about my joke.

"Alucardo," Nito echoed bitterly.

"Bye."

I hung up.

A sense of accomplishment overtook me. I smiled. I'd crushed a boy. I was officially a gringa bitch who needed her space. An American by birth, I had an Eskimo's heart. I wasn't blessed with the patience to deal with handicapped, macho Bohemians who needed love. Who did Nito think I was? Mother Teresa? No, sir. I was too busy nurturing my OCD, chewing the insides of my cheeks raw, and letting Blaze erode my lesbian cherry to worry about anyone's hurt feelings.

The Pretty Ugly Club

Unlike most Catholic high schools, Saint Michael's didn't have a uniform policy. Our dean, however, sweated to enforce the dress code she updated every September. Similar to the Constitution, the document lived and breathed, and some of our faculty, namely the elderly nuns, saw the need for certain amendments such as Rule #26: "Students must dress in a manner appropriate to and suitable to their genders," as a sign that a Biblical day of reckoning was rapidly approaching.

Being a good goth under this tyrannical code was truly (pardon the overused analogy) like being MacGyver. I had severely limited resources which I had to blend to make a bang. Not even on Valentine's Day, a day of love and harmony and martyrdom, did my oppression lift. Second period, over the intercom, the school secretary summoned me to the dean's office: "Desiree Garcia, please report to Miss Hogan's. Desiree Garcia, please repot to Miss Hogan's." I dragged from Health, through the halls, down to the main office, where I entered the dean's room and took a seat in an uncomfortable, pleather chair, facing her.

The ogress in charge of discipline sat behind her wood paneled desk, smirking. She popped two white Tic Tacs into a mouth that looked like the hole at the center of a glazed donut and sucked. Her small chin came to rest on the palm of her chubby hand, and she squinted at me. In her raw, smoker's voice, the interrogation began.

"Where on earth did you get those?"

I smiled self-consciously and touched the black leather suspenders I was wearing. My thumb grazed the silver near my right boob, the buckle being attached to one of the two straps that plunged over my shoulders and met at the center of my back, connecting to a large metal ring. At the bottom of it, a single strap stretched and clipped to my waistband, making the suspenders' three leather pieces look like a "Y" held together by an "O."

The dastardly ring had been the main reason I'd picked the sadomasochistic contraption. It had a sturdy appeal, like something a dominatrix could lift me by before throwing me onto her Catherine Wheel.

"I got these in LA," I responded. "These," I cleared my throat, "were a reward."

"A reward?"

"Yeah. Didn't you see the honor roll? My name was on it. My parents rewarded me with a hundred dollar shopping spree. You know, an incentive? I begged my dad to take me to Melrose. Where all the cool shops are. Near Hollywood. My favorite store there's Retail Slut. My dad, he waited outside while I shopped."

The dean shook her head back and forth and back and forth. She sucked her mints and shook her head some more and puckered her mouth.

"Am I getting detention? Trash duty? You know, technically, I'm not breaking any rules. The dress code says nothing about bondage suspenders."

"Bondage suspenders?" she echoed.

I nodded.

The dean looked at me gravely. "I don't think punishment will help. Just go. Get back to class. And keep up the good work. The honor roll."

I nodded and left, and with that exchange, the dean and I developed an understanding. I had tacit carte blanche to go forth and dress as dreadfully as I wanted to, as long as I almost but didn't quite break any of her thirty-one rules.

Blaze loved my suspenders.

She fondled the buckles and yanked me by the silver O-ring like a butch should.

A butch.

That's what she was, although I was ignorant about the proper terminology back then. I was a femme and a dutiful one, too. I stroked Blaze's ego when it got hurt, like when guys yelled from their monster trucks, "Paa-aaat! What the fuck are you! Make up your mind!" and threw empty beer cans at her.

I knew better than those dumb boys. I knew what Blaze could do. She was dangerous with her fingers and her tongue, and intuition told me to keep her away from St. Mike's other alterna-girls, the mod who rode her dented Italian scooter to school, the born again Christian who wore jeans under her dresses and listened to religious heavy metal. I forgot about the public high school girls, though. My threat ended up coming from there.

Hannah Hills. She was the one who stole my Blaze. The humiliation slew me. My lover boi dumped me—the gothest girl in the county—for a blonde John Lennon fan, a paisley enthusiast who stank like bargain bin patchouli.

By Santa Bonita standards, Hannah Hills was famous, a local celebrity, the type of looker people in small towns fawn over because it's not a stretch to picture them on the cover of *Seventeen*. Our own skunkish Grace Kelly, fusty old white broads probably imagined phoning their friends and telling them, "Oh, before she won that Oscar, she used to cut fabric down at The Craft Barn! Ain't that a kick?"

When news spread that Hannah had "turned gay," guys had their own reactions. "That piece of ass?" I heard a jock lament. "What a waste! Gimme half an hour with her." He pumped his meaty hips. "I could bring her back..."

Blaze brought Hannah to campus to make a point, show her off. With her new trophy on her arm, she climbed the concrete steps by the student lot. Blaze and her blonde glided past the closed attendance window and up the breezeway and, because school had let out about twenty minutes earlier, campus was fairly empty.

The varsity cheer squad practiced on the outdoor stage. The janitor, Henry, pushed his squeaky cart up the hallway, past a row of lockers. Gaping from a wood bench near the news kiosk, I watched my ex parade Santa Bonita's prettiest honky past the chapel.

At Blaze's locker, they stopped. Horror of horrors, a make out session began, and I had a perfect view of their profiles. Tongues darted into the wrong mouths, and I could tell by how cheeks were undulating that they were dancing around in those wet cavities like tortured earthworms. Spit collected and glimmered at their lip corners, and Blaze put her hand on Hannah's slender hip, holding it there, steady, gentle.

This felt like a cutting gone all wrong. The razor had slipped, gone in too deep. I was losing too much blood. I was being drained. I watched Hannah pull away from Blaze and bat her eyelashes. Blaze wiped her wet mouth with the cuff of a dead man's cardigan. I looked at Hannah's t-shirt. The *Imagine* album logo.

Imagine.

I imagined killing Hannah, ripping out her hair, yanking her teeth out one by one with pliers, making a necklace out of them. I hated this Aryan maiden. She had a tan. I was so devoted to my subculture I covered my face with veiled pillbox hats intended for old crones to wear to their husbands' funerals. I wore gloves even. In California. And who was I dropped for? A bitch who collected tie-dye.

Since Malice's loyalties were with her big sis, she dumped me, too. The double breakup included no friendship alimony, so bit by bit, I worked at rekindling my ties with a trio I'd casually chilled with at the beginning of freshman year but who really became my homies post-divorce.

Laura was this group's ringleader. She was half Puerto Rican, half Costa Rican, big-boned, big-eyed, and manic depressive. Back during freshman year, Laura's ups and downs had bought her a whole month's time at this famous state mental hospital by the sea, and she'd emerged from the visit with an aura of worldliness bestowed on her. This *One Flew Over the Cuckoo's Nest* variety wisdom combined with the audacious shit that came out of her mouth were why we chose to follow her.

Sue, Laura's blonde but not as clever sidekick, had gone to the same nuthouse the same year but for a shorter stay and for a different reason. Sue got sent away because she chased a whole bunch of allergy medication down with whiskey supposedly because she was real disgusted by herself. According to the rumor mill, Sue'd gotten the hots for her own dad, and when she went out to help him on his ostrich ranch one hot October weekend, she got him drunk, seduced him in the barn, and told him, "I'm gonna make you a grandbaby."

Now how could anybody know a detail like that? "I'm gonna make you a grandbaby?" The story smacked of fiction, tall tale-ishness, wispy cotton candy gossip, the stuff of legend. Regardless of whether or not it was true, Sue was our school slut. The only thing guys had to whisper in her ear was, "You look like Alicia Silverstone, that girl from *Clueless*," and they'd have her spread-eagle in no time.

Candace rounded out the gang. She attended St. Mike's in spite of her Mormonism, and though she was a sweet, sweet girl, Candace was awful for my OCD. Zit pustules covered her chin and pinkish Braille clusters spread around her lips in whole paragraphs. I got this idea that if I stood too close to her, her skin troubles would spread to me. To avoid falling prey, I carried a decontamination stash around in my backpack.

Everyday, during all my odd periods, I excused myself to the restroom, hauling my kit with me. Standing at the sink furthest from the door, I unpacked my cotton balls, my bottle of rubbing alcohol, and my bottle of witch hazel. I held my fluffy white tufts over the basin till they dripped with tonic and then swabbed my face with their astringent power. Coolness licked my cheeks and chin, and I felt the bacteria teeming in my pores zapped.

I vowed never to become a human petri dish like Candace, and while I did remain zit free, my skin turned positively Saharan. A molting process began. Cracked, the top layer of my face lifted and sloughed off in flaky chunks. Hiss. I was a snake. A reptile. A new, smoother me slithered forth for all St. Mike's to see.

Now, given that two of my three new buddies were certified lunatics and the third belonged to a sect that wore holy underwear, they weren't much put off by my quirks. They enabled my madness, giving me reassurance when I asked, "Is my face turning lopsided?" or "Hey, did I just bump into a leper?" Instead of mocking me when I couldn't help but bunny twitch my nose, they sputtered, "Aw! How cute! She's ready for Easter!"

According to the Chinese calendar I had hanging above my bed, 1992 was the Year of the Monkey. For me, it was the Year of the Crazy

Girl. I watched us attack people on TV talk shows, heard about us aiding and abetting our husbands' sex crimes. In Hollywood, we rose to power as madams. Amy Fisher became our queen.

One afternoon, on my front porch, me, Laura, Sue and Candace took turns reenacting the shooting of Mary Jo Buttafuco. We did it democratically, making sure each of us got a chance to ring the doorbell and shoot our nemesis point blank in the face, and later, at Laura's house, we created Amy: The Long Island Lolita, a five-act play starring Barbies. The love story ended with Skipper, shorn bald, slurring, "I'll always love my Joey...no mattah what." In the background, a pink Corvette rocked. Ken, with his pants around his ankles, plugged away at brunette Rocker Barbie, a.k.a. Amy, in the backseat.

So inspired were we that when Laura's front door opened and then slammed shut hard, we all gave a start. Laura's mom, looking haggard and bedraggled, stomped into the den. She leaned against the wet bar and scowled at the Barbie Dream House that sat on the floor. A long day's work at Take It E-Z, the retirement home where she nursed the living dead into their graves, had really tuckered her out.

"Laura! I hate dose new beaches dey hired!" she whined. "Frech out of ehigh eschool!" She kicked off her white shoes and set her stethoscope by a bottle of gin. "Dey duhn know hwat dair doin'! Dey duhn know how to even echange Depents!"

"Aw, poor Mommy," Laura cooed. "Why don't you change into something more comfortable and fix yourself a snack? We'll put on a show for you!"

Her mom shrugged, "All eright." Off she humped to her bedroom.

About fifteen minutes later, Laura's mom returned wearing nothing but a long thin t-shirt. It had a frog with sexy lashes waving a Puerto Rican flag, the slogan "100% Boricua" below it. In her right hand, Laura's mom was clutching one of those Happy Meal collectible cups I'd so coveted when I was little. Hers had a faded violet Grimace on it and was three-quarters filled with clear liquid.

"Sit down, Mommy!" Laura said. "Take a load off. Hit it, girls!"

Laura's mom melted into the couch, and on the chipped coffee table, we staged a performance of our play. At first, we thought our audience hated it. Act V closed and Laura's mom sat wordless. Then, she began to cheer. I noticed her drink was half gone.

"Otra!" she insisted. "Otra! Encore!"

We gladly re-staged our magnum opus for her, and the second time it ended, Laura's mom urged, "Cam here, my gairls! Cam here!"

We gathered around her on the couch, her short tan legs not quite reaching the floor, and she passed her glass to each of us. She watched us gulp our small reward, a toxic sip. I winced as my swallow went down, and Laura's mom looked on me dotingly, a mother hen. My throat burned. I wasn't at all used to vodka.

Candace's house wasn't as fun as Laura's. There was no liquor cabinet, no Ronald McDonald cups filled with funny stuff, but we still hung out there sometimes, regardless. Candace insisted.

Since her mom suffered from Chronic Fatigue Syndrome, the lady never got out of bed. In fact, none of us ever actually saw her face. Just her feet. Her presence was like that of the Mighty Oz. Candace would go ask her something, and the rest of us would hover by the door, hearing the conversation, the door open enough for us to glimpse framed Bible verses on the wall, the Book of Mormon on the dresser, the palest feet and calves ever poking out at the foot of the bed, resting on a delicate quilt.

We had fun with Candace's mom's yearbooks. Candace hauled them out one day, blew the dust off one's jacket, cracked it open. She held the book up and displayed a page to us, and she pointed to a black and white senior portrait. It was a young man who looked like a pigeon in a suit.

"Guess who that is," Candace prompted.

I squinted and read the boy's name aloud, "Vincent Fournier. So?"

Candace cleared her throat. I noticed a papule on her neck. I had to go swab my face. Immediately.

Candace sang, "School's out for summer!"

I forgot about my ritual.

Me and Laura and Sue shrieked, "Alice Cooper!"

"Yup. My mom went to school with him. Look what it says in his senior notes."

We quietly read them to ourselves.

"Jesus Christ almighty!" said Laura. "His dream came true. He really did become a major recording artist. That poor fucker, though. He looked like the biggest dork ever."

"Uh-huh," I agreed. "He sure did."

We passed the yearbook around, each of us touching Vince's picture, hoping some of his star power would rub off.

Home a few hours later, I swabbed my face with astringents for a good thirty minutes to make up for what I'd skipped at Candace's and then some. Once my skin felt too tight, I screwed the cap back onto my rubbing alcohol and left the bathroom and went to my bedroom to hit the books. I worked hard to keep my grades up in order to keep my parents off my back, and for Mom and Dad, decent marks meant nothing below Bs. Also, they expected me to go to a good college so I cheated a little at math to get the kind of GPA the University of California was scouting for. History and English weren't problems, though. I enjoyed doing that homework.

Stretched out on my carpet, I opened *The Scarlet Letter* and read, fantasizing that Hester Prynne was a young Mexican girl who wore a black sweater with a red "M" on it. The phone rang.

"Desiree!" my ten-year-old sister, Libertad, yelled out. "It's Nito!"

My forehead wrinkled. I hadn't heard from the kid in months. I set my book down, walked to my parents' room, and picked up the receiver.

"Bueno?" I heard Libertad hang up the other line.

"Hola."

"What's up?"

"I am only a few hours away. In Ventura. I am on my way to see you."

"What!?"

"I am in Ventura. I am on my way to see you."

"You can't! No one invited you!"

"I have your address. I will be there tomorrow. See you when you get out of school."

Click.

I slammed down the phone and screamed, "Mooooom! Mooooom! Mooo-my!" I stormed into the family room. Mom was sitting on the couch, grading papers, drinking a glass of wine. "Mom!" I announced. "Nito's on his way here!"

She set down her goblet. "Que?"

"That was Nito. He says he's in Ventura and he's coming here tomorrow!"

Mom looked confused. "Hmm. I'll go call Fe. We'll find out what's going on."

Mom walked to her room, shut her door, and called her sister. Thirty minutes later, armed with the scoop, she came and found me in my room. Mom sat on the bed across from me, and while I wove a nervous tapestry with my hair, she spared me no detail. "Fe says you broke Nito's heart," she admonished. "He traveled to the jungle in Oaxaca on a spiritual quest because of this. His father, of course, did not approve of it, and so he cut him off." Mom paused. "While Nito was living with the Indians, a revelation came to him. He had to come to America and find you."

I quit twirling my hair and widened my eyes.

"We can't turn him away..." Mom began.

I fumed, "But–"

"No buts! Nito is family. He's your cousin. Have pity on him. His legs, Desiree... Don't you roll your eyes at me!"

I was aghast. She was taking the mi casa es su casa[52] thing way too far. Fuck hospitality. This gimp was nuts.

DOUBLE THE RICAN, DOUBLE THE FUN. That's what the fuzzy, iron-on letters across the front of Laura's jersey spelled. Across her boobs. Her big boobs. I loved them. I liked the jersey, too. I thought it was clever.

Laura leaned up against an empty bathroom stall and spat. She shook the paper cup she gripped in her left hand, swirling the tobacco juice at the bottom.

"Nito!" she said. "That's neato! What the hell kinda name is that? It sounds like 'Neato! That's so cool! Neat!'"

"I know," I said. "You're exasperating me. Shut up about it already. Quit being facetious. It's like me pointing out you're double Rican. Duh. Puerto and Costa. Quit with the obvious. I already told you. Nito's a nickname. His real name's Nicolas."

"And he's your cousin, right?"

"Yeah," I sighed. "He's my cousin. But we're not blood-related," I emphasized. "We only made out 'cause I was drunk."

Laura raised her eyebrows suspiciously. "You are a lesbian, right?"

"Yes," I sighed. "I'm a lesbian." A Magna smoldered in my right hand.

---

52   my house is your house

110

Laura half grinned. Like a rodeo circuit cowboy, she spat more juice out the corner of her mouth, this time aiming for the toilet bowl beside her. Bull's-eye.

I checked my wristwatch, a Burger King model, part of *The Nightmare Before Christmas* series, purple jelly band, bats fluttering all over it. The digital face blinked 2:34.

"One, two, three, four," I whispered in order to complete the sequence, make it balanced, two numbers on each side. I looked up at Laura. "Hey! We've only got, like, five minutes to get back to class."

Laura sucked the last bit of zest from her chew, spat into her cup, and then reached into her gums, pulling out the hairy blob. She flicked her cud into the toilet bowl and my cigarette butt followed, sizzling as it extinguished.

"Here." Laura palmed me a slice of spearmint Wrigley's. She squirted cologne over our heads. With my heel, I flushed the incriminating evidence down the toilet, and we scurried out and back to class, Laura to Consumer Math, me to Living a Christian Lifestyle.

Human Cargo

We'd moved away from the neighborhood where the fugitive had crawled through my window so many years ago. Our newer house was in a fancy neighborhood called Pitt Hills. Dad liked standing on our porch, looking out across our homestead, reaching out his arms, and saying, "Kids, now we're living in the pits!"

Dad was a big pun man, and he pitched many a witticism that sailed right over Mom's head. I mean, with distinguishing the difference between "shit" and "sheet" giving her a hard time, Dad's word riddles were like Aramaic to her. Poor thing. It wasn't that she was stupid, though. Mom's a left-brained thinker, a Marie Curie type, a geek. She studied chemistry in Mexico and when I turned ten, she landed her dream job, joining the faculty of our local community college, Babcock. Myself, I hated science, so as far as I'm concerned, what she does all day is teach people how to look good in lab coats and how to blow shit up.

I've always appreciated Dad's right-brained tendencies. They're more in keeping with my own. Though he's a Mexican by birth, Dad came over here with his parents when he was like four so I consider him pretty American. And he loves language. Languages. Slavic ones. Germanic ones. Romance ones. Mostly, when he plays, he plays with English. Twisting it around. Having fun with it. Making up tongue twisters. Correcting Mom.

"We're not going to the bitch," he quipped at her one summer. "We're not going to see your mom. We're going to the beach!"

I laughed, "Ha, ha, ha!"

Mom scowled. She knew Dad was picking on her but it took a good thirty seconds to figure shit out. There's no need to pity Mom for being picked on like that. It's just Dad's way of teasing her to show her he loves her, same as how immature boys who like girls pull their ponytails, and Mom showed Dad how much she loved him by pulling some strings at Babcock and getting him a job there as a linguistics professor.

Because of all the new dough they raked in, they were able to get us the cherry new pad and send me to St. Mike's. That was what they valued as Chicano nerds: home and education. Both of them drove piece of shit cars, and the clothes me and Libertad and my brother Vincie wore weren't all that ritzy... but, boy, was our address and schoolin' to be envied.

The afternoon Nito arrived, I rode shotgun in Candace's Ford Escort as it pulled in through the gates of my exclusive neighborhood. To make Pitt Hills seem rustic, the streets had no sidewalks and they were lined with tall eucalyptus trees that shed big nutty seeds. The Escort drove over them and they scattered, making popping noises as they ricocheted off the chassis of the car.

Going up Donahue Drive, Sue decreed, "Desiree, your neighborhood's weird."

"I know," I said. "People do stupid things when they have too much money."

The girls looked at the estates lining my drive, most built on half-acre lots, most having their own unique, grotesque themes. To the right was one all boulders and rock, like a cave. To the left was a gray Tudor castle. Back on the right was a barn, an actual barn. Me and Dad joked that the people living there thought they were living in Hoedown Hills, not Pitt Hills.

Finally we came upon my house. It was a plain old, one story ranch style number. Ordinary. Unobtrusive. A solitary figure in a trench coat limped towards the corner house, the one whose yard was totally invaded by ice plant and bushy pampas grass. I gasped. That misshapen silhouette, I could recognize it anywhere.

Shrieks filled the car: "Oh my God, oh my God, oh my God! That's him!"

Candace drove up beside him. I rolled down my automatic window. Nito stooped and hunched a little to look at me.

Like he was deaf, Laura screamed, "Que pasa[53]?" from the backseat.

"The police came," he said to her. "They told me to leave so I—"

"Don't talk to them," I commanded Nito. "They don't speak Spanish. Not even the one who just asked 'Que pasa?' Why'd they call the police? What were you doing?"

"I was sitting on your lawn. Reading. Meditating."

I felt a tiny pang of solidarity with my cousin. Our white neighbors had spied a Mexican with a knapsack studying Hegel on our grass. Highly suspicious. Better nip this in the bud now or soon there'd be drive-bys.

"Get in," I said.

Laura opened the back door and Nito crowded in beside her.

---

53   What's up?

Because he stank, we collectively held our breaths. Candace made a U-y back to my house, pulling up the long, steep driveway, and parked underneath the basketball hoop. Doors opened and we got out and everyone trudged to the porch. I let us in. Quietly, we filed into the family room. I led the way to a couch and Laura and Sue and Candace bunched onto it with me. Nito was forced to sit alone on the opposite sectional. Our coffee table, stained by coffee rings and littered by Time magazines, separated us. A no man's land.

I reached for the remote and turned on the TV. The Ricki Lake Show. It would get us through this ordeal. The female members of that afternoon's guest panel were trying to figure out who their babies' daddies were. DNA testing and accusations of "You a ho! You a ******* ho!" filled the silence till Mom got home.

When she saw Nito, she did the unspeakable. She hugged him. Though we'd offered him a ride up our driveway, we were all still trying to maintain a safe distance. He smelled damn funny. Like sand and foot. Like maybe he hadn't bathed since Tijuana.

"How did he get here?" Mom asked me.

I looked at Nito. He was sitting with his legs cocked askew, the soles of both his feet placed flat on the ground. I turned to Mom and shrugged. It was a fair question. We lived about five miles out of town, beside a winery. Considering his condition, Nito couldn't have walked here.

Nito turned and opened the satchel beside him, fishing for something. We watched him pull out a stale piece of bread. He began nibbling at the crust.

"Nito?" Mom asked. "Would you like something to eat?"

"No, no," he said. "This is fine." He turned to look at me. He set his bread down on his knee. "Desiree, I have a gift for you."

Laura buried her face in her knees and giggled.

Nito dug back in his bag and tenderly pulled out a small, black velvet pouch. He handed it to me. His wet eyes looked eager for me to open it.

I took the bag from him and pulled open the drawstrings and slid the contents into the palm of my hand. Two opal earrings, shaped like pregnant teardrops, glimmered. I glanced back at Nito. He was waiting for some sort of thanks. Maybe a hug. A kiss. Or a peck.

"Gracias," I said. "See you later."

I turned and made a beeline for my room. I heard footsteps behind me, my girls, my gang.

I pulled out my shiny black chair from under my shiny black desk and angled it so I was facing Laura and Sue, who sat side by side, on my shiny black bed. I lowered myself onto the hard chair and glanced down at Candace. She was sitting on the floor, reclining with her palms flat against my carpet. The damn spot would require disinfection later on.

"Your cousin's a weirdo," pronounced Sue.

"Tell me about it," I said.

"You know he wants a kiss," Laura teased. "You've already kissed him before. Just go out there and do it. Slip him the tongue. Let him..."

"Shut—"

Mom rapped three warning knocks on my door but didn't wait for an answer. She barged right in. I glared at her for not waiting for my permission, but she marched directly up to me and stood, arms akimbo. In English, so that all my friends could hear her, she reprimanded, "Desiree, joo hab hitten in here too long! Nito eez joor guest. Go aut dair ant be a betairr hostess."

"But, Mommy!" I wailed. "I didn't invite him!"

"So ghwat! He's fameely. He cayim oll dis way to see you. Go aut der ant spent some tayeem weet him!"

Laura chuckled.

I mad-dogged her. Mom spun around and left.

Sighing, I peeled myself off my chair and plodded back to the family room. My cronies followed. I saw Nito huddled into the corner of the same long sectional sofa. From her armchair, Mom gestured for me to join him. I frowned, and sat at the opposite end of the sofa. Laura, Candace, and Sue clustered around me. The boy-girl polarity created a lopsided, teeter-totter effect.

Laura waved at Nito and blustered, "Ahoy!"

Nito looked me straight in the eye and whispered, "Hola."

Mom drank some wine and drummed her fingers on the arm of her chair. She'd changed *Ricki Lake* to CNN and was watching *Crossfire*. Two enraged political pundits debated on the small screen, and a stare down between Nito and my camp got underway.

"Why don't you try on the earrings?" Nito asked, in search of a checkmate.

"Later," I replied.

Stalemate.

The stare down continued.

Dad came home at 6. We sat down at the kitchen table to eat, and since Libertad and Vincie were away at science camp, and I'd invited a gaggle of ingrates over, Mom had opted not to cook. Instead, she'd ordered pizza.

Sitting between Sue and Laura, I grimaced. Mom handed me a flimsy paper plate that I plunked down in front of me with disdain. I stared at the slice on it. It was covered in pepperoni and oozing. Mechanically, I began plucking off the sausage and slipping it into my napkin. Once it was meat-free, I grabbed a new napkin and pressed it to the cheese. It absorbed the bright orange grease. I peeled off the saturated paper and laid a new one down. It turned bright orange, too. I kept doing this, till Dad hissed, "Quit with the paper napkin routine and just eat your food."

I nodded and set my greasy napkins, along with the one bulging with pepperonis, on a separate plate. Suddenly my diseased subconscious radioed me a ritual. I abided by it, eating my mushrooms first, my cheese second, my saucy bread third, my crust last. I concentrated on following each step and chewing in meticulous multiples of two till my slice was gone. I refrained from any conversation because deviating even slightly from one step could've opened a Pandora's box of consequences—cancer, acne, AIDS, female baldness—that I had no way of shutting.

Nito's eating habits rivaled mine in strangeness. He refused to touch his slice of pizza, and like some kind of recently emerged desert hermit who hadn't re-assimilated to civilization yet, he hobbled to his knapsack and fished out the last of that mangy hunk of bread. Dad tried not to stare as Nito carried it back to the table and polished it off, crunching on its staleness.

"Well, we're going out now!" I announced, carrying my plate, my napkins, and my pepperonis to the trash. "We're gonna go bowling! Don't wait up for us. Mom, Dad... have fun with Nito!"

Mom stopped daubing chile onto her slice. She looked up at me and said, "Oh no, Desiree. You're taking him with you."

I fumed. I looked at Nito.

"Andale[54]!" I almost yelled.

Sue and Laura held in their laughter as we walked out to the Escort. They climbed in and let out their guffaws, and I remained, poised by the open passenger door, my arms folded across my chest, thinking.

"Candace," I suggested, "We can put Nito in the trunk. He'll fit."

She was tying a shoelace, and she looked up at me like I was joking. She pulled her knot tight and then stood up and walked to the rear of the car. She unlocked it. The lid popped open.

---

54   Hurry!

"Here?" she asked.

"Yup."

"Nito!" I called. He was loitering by a potted ficus in front of the garage. "There," I pointed at the trunk.

Dumbfounded at first, Nito soon realized I wasn't kidding. His facial expression turned to resigned disgust. With no other choice, he limped to the trunk and wriggled in. I followed him and supervised and once his body was curled snugly around the spare tire, I slammed the lid shut on him. I skipped to the passenger seat and hopped in beside Candace.

She pulled out of our driveway and drove us down Donahue Drive, out of Pitt Hills, past oil fields with massive green grasshoppers pumping crude out of the earth.

"Are you sure it's safe to put someone in the trunk?" Candace asked. "It won't kill him, will it? The fumes won't kill him, will they?"

"Your trunk looked well-ventilated," I assured her.

I gazed out the window at a ramshackle Victorian surrounded by bean fields. Two old ladies, who I suspected were dykes, lived there. One always sat on the weathered porch wearing a flower print housedress and the other, dressed like a man, always tooled around in the yard in big swamp boots.

Candace asked, "What about carbon monoxide?"

"Don't worry about it," I said.

"Are you sure?"

"Candace!" I raised my voice. "He's used to it! How do you think he got here? He probably rode to this country in somebody's trunk. Gosh."

Candace nodded.

We rode into downtown Santa Bonita and took a shortcut through the parking lot of Snappy's Stop N' Go, in through the alleyway behind Fujimori Pharmacy. We snaked around Butler Elementary School, winding past brown-shingled tract houses built at the height of tacky American home design, the early '80s. Candace lived at 500 McElhany Way, a good number, an even number with two zeroes, and she turned into her driveway, easing her Escort in beside an old Buick Skylark.

"Whose is that?" I asked.

"Paco's."

The four of us climbed out and skirted Candace's dry lawn, taking the concrete path to the front door.

"Who's Paco?"

"My brother's best friend."

"You've got a brother?" Laura asked.

"Yeah. Sammy. He got out of jail today."

Sammy must've heard us because the torn screen door flung open and we beheld the jailbird in all his stocky glory, crowned by a Black Pantheresque 'fro. Backlit by a hall light, Sammy looked almost like an angel, but as I got closer, I saw how his beady eyes twinkled behind hidden eyelids. A criminal smile spread across his face.

Candace rushed into his arms. They embraced. Sammy smiled. He was missing a canine. "Heya, sis!" he gushed. He squeezed Candace close to his chest and peeked at the rest of us from over her shoulder. "Who're these lovely ladies?"

Candace pulled away from him and turned to gesture at us. "These are my friends. From St. Mike's."

"Hi, girls."

"Hi," we chorused.

Sammy motioned for us to follow him into the house, to the den. Laura whispered, "Is the Mighty Oz asleep?"

"I don't know." Candace turned to her brother. "Sammy, is Mommy sleeping?"

He smiled and nodded and then motioned at a Mexican who I figured was Paco. The guy was seated on a blue La-Z-Boy, prepping a bong. He concentrated, studious as a schoolboy, on the task at hand. Paco was a marijuana savant.

I rubbed my palms together. "Goody, goody gumdrops," I said in an excited whisper. "After all the shit I've been through today, I could really use a smoke."

Sue poked me in the arm. "Aren't you forgetting something?"

"Oh, yeah. But, um, I have to take the first hit."

My seeming selfishness attracted Paco's attention. His cinnamon-colored eyes looked up from the purple glass contraption. "How come you gotta take the first hit?" Paco asked.

"Just 'cause," Laura defended. "It's not like Desiree's gonna hog the bowl or anything. That's just how she is." She folded her arms across her chest. "Anything that we share with our mouths, she's gotta go first. It's her habit. It makes Desiree unique."

Paco wiggled his eyebrows. "You go first with your mouth?"

"Duuuuuumb," I rebuffed. His sexual innuendo was weak.

Paco laughed and passed me the bong and a Zippo. I sparked up, took a deep toke, and let the smoke come hissing deliciously out of me.

"'Kay," I said, "I'm ready to go get the freak show out of the trunk now. Candace, gimme your keys. Laura, come with me to go get it out."

Candace tossed me her key ring, and I walked back out to the driveway with Laura. I unlocked the trunk and lifted the lid.

"Salte[55]," I commanded into the cramped, dark space.

Nito's top half emerged. We watched him awkwardly fumble the rest of his way out.

"We are at Candace's house," I told him as he got his land legs back. "Follow me."

We brought him into the smoke filled den.

---

55   Get out.

"Odelay!" Sammy called to Nito. "Wassup, dude?"

Hovering on the periphery of the ganja pow-wow, I snapped, "Sammy, don't act like you know him. He doesn't need any encouragement."

"But I do know him. We picked up this guy at the Greyhound Station today and gave him a ride out to some big house in the middle of nowhere. He's cool. Kinda serious, though."

"Sammy," I began, my tone filled with shock, "did you take him to Pitt Hills? Up a long, steep driveway? Plain white house with green shutters and a red brick porch?"

"Yup."

I beat my chest with my fist. "That's my house!"

"No way! Trip out..."

I turned to look at Paco. He was taking deep bong rip after deep bong rip. Pig. The guy looked straight up Indian. Olmec. Tarascan. Chichimeca, they of the tribe who wrangle dogs.

"Hey, Paco," I began, "did you, like, talk to Nito? Did he tell you why he's here?"

Exhaling, Paco stroked a dark, greasy lock of hair. "No se habla Español[56], man. Dude just needed a ride. So we gave him one." A mushroom cloud ensconced his head. Paco was awake but in the Land of Nod.

My face twitched, and my fingers went to my hair. I imitated Paco's hair play.

"Listen," Sammy explained to me and Laura, "while you guys were letting that dude outta the car, the rest of us came up with a plan. We decided it'd be cool to drive to Guadalupe. Paco's got some Keystone out in the Skylark. We'll have my Welcome Home party out at the dunes!"

Sue, our school's president of Students Against Drunk Driving,

---

56   No Spanish spoken.

squealed, "Yeah!"

I watched Candace polish off the bowl, her face looking the zittiest I'd ever seen it. Sammy put on his wool-lined jean jacket and sang, "Onward Christian soldiers, marching as to war..."

He marched to the door. Everyone followed.

"Andale," I said to Nito.

We were the last ones out onto the driveway where Laura was carrying a six-pack from the Buick to the Ford. Leaning against the passenger door, she tore off three shiny cans and tossed each of us a present.

"One for the road!" she said.

I cracked mine opened, foam spilled forth, and I took a swill.

After securing Nito back inside the trunk, I slammed the lid shut on him and hopped back into the passenger seat beside Candace. She drove us west, past the Indian Motor Lodge, the Happy Camper Trailer Park and Mazzini's Dairy Farm, where we'd gone when I was in third grade to watch the cows get milked. I could hear Laura and Sue in the backseat matching each sip of beer Candace and I took with a guzzle, and soon, their cans were empty.

"Mind if me and Sue finish off these last two?" Laura asked. She ripped a burp that stank up the car.

I pinched my nose.

Candace said, "Go for it."

Narrow two lane roads cutting through miles of dark strawberry fields delivered us to the shore. Laura collected our empty cans and tossed them out the window. They landed noiselessly on the sand. I could see the dunes' entrance. A thick chain blocked the one lane road. Darkness filled the guard booth. I heard an owl hoot nearby.

Candace set the parking brake. "We're in for a hike," she said.

We spilled out of the Escort and into the night and the rough ocean breeze rustled our hair. Candace took the initiative of going to the trunk to release Nito. As the lid popped open, Laura channeled Whitney Houston, belting out, "I believe that children are our future, teach them well and let them lead the way." In the darkness, Nito grasped for something to hold onto. He flopped onto the dirt, flailing. Laura pointed at his tangled mass of limbs and sang, "Show them all the beauty they possess inside..."

Paco and Sammy pulled up behind us, flashing their lights. The strobe they cast on Nito made it look like he was doing performance art, perhaps Japanese Butoh dance. Sammy killed the Skylark's engine and parked. He and Paco unloaded the cases of booze, readying them for the haul.

"Follow me," whispered Paco. "I know this place real good."

Like pack mules, they led us up a trail that took us to epic looking sand dunes. In the light of the full moon, their majesty commanded our awe. I now understood why Cecil B. DeMille had chosen to film *The Ten Commandments* here. We were Hebrews, escaping from Pharaoh.

Sammy and Paco climbed to the top of a dune, collecting twigs from a nearby grove to make a campfire. It blazed and we formed a circle around it, Candace and I starting our second drinks, Sue and Laura their fifth or sixth.

Laura moaned, "Someone's cryin' mah Lord! Kumbaya..."

She sang with her eyes shut as the rest of us watched Nito head towards a short dune three mounds down. He scurried up it and planted himself atop it, cross-legged. He stared up at the moon, its rays illuminating the angry lines in his face. He fished a beanie out of his pocket and pulled it on over his head.

Sammy said, "Your husband looks pissed."

"He's not my husband," I snapped.

"Go check on him," Sue told me. "Make sure he doesn't, like, have a knife or something and is planning on, like, hopping over here and stabbing us."

I sighed, stood up, and went to check on Nito.

Hiking up his duneside, I pretended to be cheerful. I heard Sammy begin howling. He was singing the chorus of "Paradise City." Wayward Mormon was no Axl Rose.

"How's it going?" I asked Nito.

He made me wait for his response as he gazed at the waters of the Pacific lapping at the shore.

"You are evil," he hissed.

"Okay, bye," I said and split.

As I returned to the campfire, Sammy quit singing. "What's up with the Nitster?" he asked.

"I don't know," I said. "But he's definitely pissed."

"He looks like an oracle," said Laura. "Let's go ask it for advice."

"No," I said.

We sang "Clementine" and "Oh Susannah" and did a round of "Row, Row, Row Your Boat" and since Sammy begged, "American Pie." We made fun of my cousin, drained the cases of Keystone, and shouted our throats hoarse. Two hours before dawn, Paco and Sammy threw sand on our fire, and we stumbled back to the cars. Candace drove us back through the countryside without killing us or the doe that decided to prance unexpectedly across the road, and we entered Pitt Hills in one piece.

At the top of my driveway, the Escort idled as I let Nito out of the trunk. We walked across the concrete path together, to the brick porch, and I held the front door open for him. Nito followed me down the hall, to Vincie's bedroom.

"You are sleeping in here," I said, flipping the light switch. I pointed at a twin bed dressed in He-Man sheets. "Buenas noches."

"Desiree—" I heard, but it was too late.

I'd already shut the door behind me.

I went with Dad to take Nito to the Greyhound station. Mom forced me to. I stayed by the lockers near the glass doors, watching Dad march the cripple to the ticket counter.

"Here," he told him. Dad handed him fifty bucks. "Don't come back." Stern-faced, Dad lifted his eyebrows. He was waiting for an answer.

Nito looked down at his feet. Nodded.

What a relief. At least one parent took craziness for what it was: craziness.

We stayed and watched to make sure Nito boarded a bus destined for far-off places and then Dad dropped me off at Laura's. Her front door was unlocked so I let myself in and walked to her room. I could hear giggling from the hall. I knocked on her door and pushed it open and found all three of my friends sitting on the carpet, passing around a jug of yellow Gatorade. Candace held it out to me.

"We're hydrating," she said. "Want some."

I examined her skin and shook my head and knelt on the carpet. "You guys never heard about the pee scare?" I asked.

"What pee scare?"

"A few years ago, some delivery guy peed in all these bottles of Gatorade. They shipped them all over California and people bought them and gulped down the guy's urine, and they didn't even know what they were drinking since that stuff looks like pee and tastes salty, anyways."

"Really?" Sue grabbed the bottle and sniffed the lip.

"Uh-huh."

Laura lunged at me and stopped with her face poised an inch from mine. She opened her mouth and exhaled deep. "I've been drinking this shit all afternoon. How do I smell?"

I looked at her dog, Richard, asleep in the corner. I cocked my head, "Like you've been making out with him all morning."

Laura leaned back and grinned. "Hey, how long did it take you to fall asleep last night?"

"Quick. How come?"

"I would've stayed up if I was you. Nito probably snuck into your room and stood over you while you were sleeping." She waved her hands like a sorcerer and chanted, "'She will be mine, she will be mine, she will be mine, she will—'"

"Pinche puta cabrona malcreada[57]!"

Laura cackled gleefully. She collected insults the way some kids collected coins.

"That was a good one!" she said.

"Hmph." I stood up. "I'm going to the kitchen. Does anyone want anything?"

"No."

I left and walked to the dining room. Laura's water cooler stood in the corner, behind a table with a bowl of dusty plastic fruit on it. I skirted around the chairs and pulling a Dixie cup from the beige dispenser, poured myself a drink. The Culligan man, Jim, who Sue thought was cute, had delivered the now half-empty water bottle Wednesday. I tried not to think of Jim with his dick out, peeing in all the cargo out in the back of his truck, giggling like a maniacal panty sniffer from the movies.

---

57   Fucking evil bitch

Hechizo[58]

I'd gone and let myself forget about you-know-who, and with summer less than three weeks away, I was excited. I'd have three months to do anything with. I could sit around like a tree stump all day if I wanted to. I could O.D. on Mountain Dew and twitch on the floor and pull my own hair out. I could catch dragonflies and bumble bees and hold them hostage in jars and find out how long they could live without air. ·

But first, I had to make it through June.

Candace and Sue and Laura were just as itchy as I was for school to be over and with an entire season of freedom looming, we were extra jittery, decompressing at my house, doing our usual after school routine of snacks and *Beverly Hills 90210* reruns, the good ones from before Shannen Doherty got kicked off the show. From where I was wrinkling

---

58   Spell

my nose in the family room, I could see Laura working in the kitchen. Dressed in Mom's faded red and white apron, she manned the stove. All four burners blazed, each one with a pan frying on top. Laura lifted her spatula, transforming into... Napoleon, saber raised, leading a doomed cavalry into Waterloo.

"I hope you bitches are hungry!" she called. "And don't forget! Kiss the cook!"

Sue was sitting on one of the sectionals, near Candace. She fumbled with the remote and giggled, "Ew, I don't wanna get herpes!"

"Shut up ya dumb broad!" Laura yelled. "Ya already got it! What d'ya think cold sores are?"

"Hey, I'm gonna go get the mail," I said. "Does anyone wanna come?"

Candace went limp. Sue, catatonic.

"Hmph," I sniffed.

Barefoot, I headed out the door by myself. I padded across the enclosed porch, past a trail of ants, and noticed that the June sun had really baked our driveway. The heat started to sting my soles and I moaned, "Ouch!" and flexed my feet, curving them. I crept toe to heel, toe to heel, toe to heel past the bee brigade that was pollinating the pink flowers bushes along our hillside. The insects droned loud and angry. I hoped my presence wouldn't offend them.

Reaching the last shrub, I inched around it, extra careful, stepping out onto the curb. I raised my arms to help me catch my balance and looked down at the gutter. It was a thicket of bugs, leaves and clay. I couldn't fall into that cesspool. Imitating a tightrope walker, I took a few steps forward. With the mailbox two feet in front of me, I threw myself at it, grabbing it, using it to steady myself with.

Opening the lid, I peered inside. The mailman had delivered a healthy stash. I pulled it out, shut the lid, and tightrope walked back to the driveway.

Round two of toe to heel, toe to heel started, and I sorted through credit card offers Dad would put through his shredder, bills Mom would whip out the checkbook to pay. I wondered where to hide my overdue notices from the library and decided that I was going to have first crack at Dad's *National Geographic* and Mom's book club catalogue.

The final piece of mail was a medium-sized manila envelope addressed only to, "Ella[59]." I stopped and stared at it. The return address said the letter was sent from the resident of a plain sounding street in Vacaville. They'd omitted their name. I examined the handwriting. Shaky. Someone was trying to disguise their penmanship.

I ripped the envelope open, unleashing a dessert smell, sweet as fresh bile. Nervous, I braced myself and stuck my hand in the envelope. The surprising texture of tissue paper. I sat down in the middle of the driveway and held my breath and tipped the envelope. A four by six sheet slid out onto my lap. A plagiarized title, "Les Fleurs Du Mal[60]," was printed across the top. Below it, a Spanish ode was written in cursive slanted to the left. The anonymous poem's subject was a girl, a mean one who was going to get hers.

I thought back to the night at the dunes. "Desiree," I echoed, "you are evil." Goosebumps erupted across my backside.

I rested the poem on my thigh and reached back into the envelope, sliding something else out. It was a circle made of tissue paper, burnt along its edges. Writing began along the periphery and wound, like a coiled snake, into nothing at the center.

I tried to but couldn't make out the alphabet. It wasn't Indo-European. Not Asian. I guessed it wasn't African either. What in the hell was this thing? A psycho wheel that smelled like little girl lip gloss?

It smacked of magic.

I shoved the circle and poem back into the envelope, rose, and,

---

59   Her.
60   The Flowers of Evil

like a firewalker, sprinted up the driveway. Storming into my house, I marched into the family room. Sue, Laura and Candace were lying on the couches. They were shoveling Mexican food into their faces with the top buttons of their jeans undone.

I glanced at the TV. Brenda Walsh was in a panic. The teenage heroine had discovered a lump in her breast and was waiting for the biopsy results.

"Look at this shit!" I thundered. Everyone gave a start. I tossed the envelope onto the coffee table. Candace, Sue, and Laura set down their plates and huddled around it. "Look at it!"

They spent five minutes in silence, examining the envelope and its contents.

"Desiree!" Laura finally boomed. "That's the scariest fucking thing I've ever seen!"

"I know! It's voodoo," I accused. "Santeria!"

"What're you gonna do?" asked Sue.

"I know what we should do," Candace suggested. "We should take it to Rex. T-Rex."

"The warlock?" Sue asked.

"The warlock," she nodded.

I'd been to The Apothecary before, with Blaze and Malice.

Its proprietor, T-Rex, ran the shop out of a failing strip mall near the bridge. He never had much merchandise, mostly he peddled crystal meth out the back door, but Malice had enjoyed hanging out there, listening to T-Rex sing Rasputin's praises, browsing through what little he had. Daggers with long white blades. Pouches made of chain mail. Chalices. Incense. Pricey Renaissance Fair costumes and accessories.

The day after my esoteric package arrived, me and my friends bustled in through The Apothecary's glass door. Small brass bells hanging from the handle clinked together, chiming. I spotted T-Rex, sitting on the counter, next to the register. He was tearing tin foil off a burrito and swaying to some Celtic beats, probably Dead Can Dance. With his teeth, he tore open a chile packet and took a chomp out of his burrito, injecting it with hot sauce.

A punk dressed and made up to look like Nancy Spungeon sat on a folding chair in the corner. A notebook was spread open across her lap, tic-tac-toe games covering its pages. Filthy nails reached up to scratch her neck.

"Cat's game..." she said.

What a tweaker.

I looked over my shoulder. Oh, God. From the way Candace was carrying on, you wouldn't have guessed it was her idea to come here. She was clinging to Sue's arm like she was a buoy in a typhoon. Sue stood, frozen and wide-eyed, by the didgeridoo-packed sale rack near the exit.

A black cat leapt onto the counter.

Candace shrieked, "Eeeeee!" and Sue screamed "Ohmigod! Ohmigod! Ohmigod!"

I looked at T-Rex apologetically. He shrugged. He was probably used to this sort of thing. Regardless, I felt it necessary to somehow chastise my companions.

"Fucking white girls," I mouthed to Laura.

"You said it!" she roared.

T-Rex didn't wig us out, and I knew that most of the melodrama behind me had to do with color: The warlock was one of the few black men in town. T-Rex's skin tone matched Mom's mestiza[61] shading, cafe con leche, Folgers with a shot of Carnation cream. My friends were caught in a black panic and that T-Rex's moustache and goatee were groomed identical to Anton La Vey's didn't help matters any.

To me, the low tide on T-Rex's head made him seem less menacing.

---

61   European and Spanish

His hairline receded so that his longish fluff sculpted out into a Bozo the Clown frame. He wore a faded Einstürzende Neubauten t-shirt that fit his pot belly snug, and at his shins, a pair of black leather things that Puss In Boots would've had designs on swallowed his jeans.

Slurp. T-Rex sucked salsa and sour cream off his fingers. Silver rings adorned them, each one displaying something a little more sinister than the next. A skull. A tarantula. A pentagram. A Chinese fingernail guard with a long, dangerously sharp tip.

I cleared my throat.

"What can I help you with today?" T-Rex asked.

Laura took his request as a cue to stretch her arms, yawn, and lean both elbows against a glass counter with a big handwritten sign taped to the front that said, "I am not your friend. DO NOT LEAN ON ME." T-Rex smirked at her.

Laura pressed her face close to the glass and examined the herbs in the case. "Hmm. Eye of newt. I wonder if Neato used any of that shit on you."

I began blinking nervously and grinding my teeth.

With the tip of his nail guard, T-Rex combed through his little beard.

I placed my envelope on the clean glass before me, swallowed, and said, "I got this weird thing in the mail, yesterday. I think I've figured out what it is, but I thought I should come here to get an expert opinion."

My ego stroking worked. T-Rex straightened up and smiled. He set his burrito down on a paper bag and turned to the tweaker.

"Michelle," he commanded, "fetch me a Coke. Lots of ice."

The girl tucked her pen in her notebook, shut it, and slid it under her chair. "Sure, big daddy," she said and trotted out the door. Small bells chimed.

T-Rex eased himself off the counter. He strode up to the package. "Now what've we got here?" He reached his right hand into the envelope and teased out the two papers. He examined them.

We all concentrated, watching him.

"This one," T-Rex finally declared, pointing at the poem, "is a bunch of horse shit. It's of no consequence. Don't worry about it."

I was relieved.

"But this one," he knocked the wheel with his knuckle, "this one's a love spell."

To the best of my knowledge, this was the first time anyone had ever cast a spell on me. I wasn't sure how to feel. Scared? Annoyed? In love?

I asked, "How does it work?"

"I'm not certain about all the particulars of this one, but I can tell you a few things about it. First, do you smell that scent?"

I nodded.

"Okay, that's some sort of rose oil. Once you get it on your fingers, you're fucked. You carry that scent with you, and it works to constantly remind you of him." He paused. "Who is he?"

In a small voice, I answered, "My cousin."

T-Rex raised his bushy eyebrows. His lips turned into a half smile. It gave him a roguish dimple. "Well, your cousin wants total control over your mind, heart, body, and soul." He pointed to the flaking, ashy edges of the wheel. "See this?"

I nodded.

"This is how the spell is activated, by burning the edges of this wheel once it's been anointed with oil. This writing that begins on the edges and spirals into the center represents something eternal. A spell that's supposed to last forever. But I can't tell you what this says. What is your cousin?"

Blank stare.

"Is he a Wiccan? Is he... What is he?"

"We're Mexican. He's from Mexico."

"Mm-hmm."

"He's, um, kinda what they call 'un hippie' there. His parents are rich. They're jewelers. He used to work for them, but, he, like, went on some kinda mission down to Oaxaca."

T-Rex nodded. "Southern Mexico. Yucatan peninsula."

"Yeah. I think he went into the jungles there to meet the sages. Get loaded and, like, hallucinate and meet God and stuff. He was always talking about doing that."

T-Rex's demeanor turned serious. "There are some very powerful shamans down there. Those guys make all this," he waved his hand, "look like child's play."

T-Rex checked me out, eyes sweeping across my frame. I'd dressed extra death bunny since it was the weekend. T-Rex's eyes sparkled. He liked what he saw.

"Did your cousin— What's his name?"

"Nito."

"Did Nito have the opportunity to collect any of your... juices?"

I heard gasps coming from behind me. Laura pretended to be ignoring us. She didn't even look up from the copy of the *Malleus Maleficarum* she'd plucked off a rack.

"Just spit," I answered and felt a panic coming on. What if Nito had HIV and had infected me with saliva that had microscopic blood particles in it? Fuck. When I got home, I was going to have to call the AIDS hotline and hash this out with a volunteer. I'd bawl. I was already having visions of myself in a coffin, Mom wondering what to do with all my things.

T-Rex stared at me while I ruminated. "Well," he said, "if he did get his hands on any of your secretions, this spell will be very hard to break."

"All he got was spit," I whispered.

T-Rex looked at me like he still didn't believe me.

"One last thing," he added, "you know that spells have a strong psychological component, right?"

"Kind of."

"Spells," T-Rex began, like he was lecturing dummies in Magic 101, "get into your head, like a virus. They infect your thoughts. Especially love spells. The whole point of one, psychologically speaking, is to trick you. You get something like this wheel," his fingertips tapped it, "and you begin wondering. You get scared. The memory of it stays with you, and the intention is to get you to ask, 'If I'm thinking so much about this and about so-and-so, am I in love with them?' It's a mind fuck. That's a lot of what magic is. Mental manipulation."

Laura looked at me over the top her book. She teased, "Desiree's gonna be a zombie," in singsong.

T-Rex silenced her with a glare.

"If I were to pay you to undo this thing," I began, "how much would it cost me?"

"Let's see." T-Rex stroked his goatee. "That would entail labor, ingredients, energy. Hmm. Good question. About a hundred dollars."

I had that much in my piggy bank, but there was no way I was wasting it to break a spell. I'd been saving up for months to buy a pair of white Doc Martin boots I'd asked for but hadn't gotten from Santa.

"I don't have that kind money," I lied, hoping T-Rex wasn't clairvoyant, too.

"Alright." He struck a bargaining pose. "How about seventy-five?"

I shook my head and opened my purse. I dug out all the spare change I could muster, about a dollars worth, and dropped it into a jar marked, "OFFERINGS."

"Thanks," I said reluctantly.

"Yup."

I scooped up my juju, turned, and left.

I tore pictures of Isabella Rossellini, Sophia Loren, and Siouxsie Sioux from magazines and taped them on the wall above my bed. I lusted after each and every one of them and masturbated to them at night.

Thank God, I was still a homosexual. Nito's spell hadn't eroded my gayness so my anxiety about the wheel lifted. Anger replaced it. I mean, how offensive to think I'm that easy. Abracadabra, wave a magic wand, slaughter a rooster, and I'm yours?

No effing way.

My self-righteous lesbian indignation, not to mention the fact that I'd saved a hundred bucks, made me smug. I was immune to hexes, but if what T-Rex had explained was true, I was enamored of some pretty sick shit. My mental illness worked exactly how he'd described the mindfuck of a spell: I could be 99.9% certain of something, but if a .01% possibility of it being false existed, that was what hooked me. Doubts haunted most of my waking hours, their shadows trumping all logic, and the sick part of my brain was so excessively rational, so excessively logical, it used the scientific method on minutiae to fuck me six ways to Sunday everyday.

Like walking to my bedroom, I imagined Nito harvesting strawberries in Watsonville or picking peaches in Fresno, maybe mopping floors in San Jose. He'd be wondering, "Is it working? Is it working?"

I laughed but then stopped in my tracks, breaking out into a sweat.

I was pretty sure I'd forgotten to tap the doorframe twice while crossing the threshold.

My favorite crooner, Morrissey, was celibate. And so I became. For him, it was about hiding from his fans that he was a fag. For me, it was about avoiding death and ruin. Babies. I couldn't shake the thought that I might be pregnant with one.

The idiocy started one afternoon senior year when the end of lunch bell rang. I was under so much pressure filling out college apps and writing bullshit personal essays that I walked around feeling like a balloon sailing towards a needle. St. Mike's halls were flooded with kids rushing to get their books from their lockers, and amid the scramble to get to fifth period on time, a boy in a letterman jacket and shorts crashed into me.

With unteenlike politesse, he offered, "That was my fault. I'm sorry."

I nodded.

My face was blue.

I'd eaten three snack bar taquitos for lunch and was struggling to hold in some nasty gas. My colon taunted me but I would not let my sphincter turn spastic. I walked carefully to my locker. As I pulled my Bible out of it, my OCD co-opted my indigestion. It became ammo and I ceased having anything as innocent as mild food poisoning. I'd been knocked up.

In my mind's eye, I saw how it'd happened. A series of mental pictures, reminiscent of mid-century Sex Ed films, illustrated the miracle of life as it'd unfolded in my womb. One of my eggs had sat placidly by as one of the athlete's rugged swimmers had fertilized it. Cells had teemed, multiplying, and our fetus swam, now a happy tadpole. My nausea was recast as morning sickness. But wait. It was too early for that. Had other guys bumped into me? Had I been the unwitting participant in a gang rape of sorts?

Yes. Of course. In the school hallways. Any one of the boys sailing down the cement paths might've had come on their flies and here they were crashing into girls and rubbing up against them, impregnating them. My baby's father could've been a freshman, a sophomore, a junior, a senior. Who knew when the impregnation had happened, and only a DNA test could tell me for sure who he was. But how to convince the entire male student body to submit to mass swabbing?

Resigned to waiting for my period, I gave myself weekly pregnancy tests. I didn't trust the little pee sticks very much, so to be on the safe side, I made Candace chauffeur me to Planned Parenthood. A couple of times. Six. We became well-informed about my options—abortion, adoption, or keeping my child—so much so that we could've counseled the expectant young mothers packing the waiting room. It was forever full. Santa Bonita High boasted the highest teen pregnancy rate in America.

My AIDS hysteria kept me busy, too. On a warm afternoon, I recklessly guzzled water from a rusty campus drinking fountain. My taste buds detected something tainted and metallic, possibly iron tinged. Wait, blood had iron. The water supply was contaminated with blood! Someone with AIDS and a bloody nose had dripped into it and now I was carrying the human immunodeficiency virus.

While thoughts of my own death usually bombarded me, panic about infecting my family with HIV terrorized me this time around. Anxiety gave me constant diarrhea and I lost ten pounds. Mom couldn't figure out why I insisted eating off paper plates and using plastic utensils. It was to avoid infecting her and Dad and Libertad and Vincie. I catalogued my symptoms on gum wrappers, napkins, and Post-its, and by the time my college acceptance letters arrived, I'd amassed an entire desk drawer full of scraps with phrases like "purple lesions," "coated tongue," and "bloody stool."

My obsessions collided at the senior lawn, this stupid patch of grass that St. Mike's soon-to-be alums earned the privilege of sitting on. Husky football players guarded its perimeter like Rottweilers, and after a really bad pep rally, I plopped down with my friends on its northwest corner to eat three of those *Soylent Green* taquitos I still hadn't learned to say no to.

Damp grass soaked my skirt. My butt got wet. Pale, I turned to Laura. "Was anyone sitting here before we got here?"

"Yeah."

"Who?"

"Jesse Lee."

Jesse Lee, a blonde surfer/stoner who God had created in the image of Jeff Spicoli. I was sure that while sitting in my spot, he had come in his pants. Some of it probably leaked through his crotch and fertilized the lawn. I'd absorbed the leftovers, his semen soaking through my skirt and panties. It was what was making my crotch moist.

And how Jesse loved drugs. He did enough of them to put him in the high-risk category for AIDS. Because of him, I wasn't just going to have a bastard—I was going to have an AIDS baby! This called for an after-school trip to the county health department.

Candace drove me there, and as a young nurse drew my blood, I told her, "Check me out for everything." I bit my nails and tapped my heel like jackhammer and twitched my mouth. "Wait!" I screamed. "I didn't see you uncap that needle!"

With her brow furrowed, the nurse stared at me. "Honey," she began, "have you been... are you being molested?"

I shook my head.

"Are you sure? You can tell me," she coaxed.

I shook my head.

She looked at me incredulously. "Well, come back in seven days for your results." She handed me some paperwork. "Bring this with you." The nurse looked at me hard, but I made out sympathy in her eyes. "Can I give you a hug?"

I nodded, but grimaced, horrified as she embraced me. I knew where her hands had been.

I, the Night Stalker, Sort of

The Thursday I found out I was HIV-negative, our dishwasher broke. And I graduated.

The dishes piled up for two nights, and me and Mom finally got around to them Saturday. We tried to have fun doing them the old-fashioned way, and I watched Mom's veiny hands hold a yellow plate as old as me under the faucet, rinsing the suds off. She glanced at me as I dried an orange Tupperware cup with a dishrag. Setting the cup on the cabinet shelf, I turned to reach out to Mom for the plate. A two second image of me pulling down her pants, ramming my fist up her vagina, and snapping her neck raced through my head.

Hold on. Where on God's green earth had that come from? Was it a flashback from a movie? Maybe a scene from that de Sade book I'd peeked into at the library?

Uh-uh. I couldn't place this violence. It was mine.

I looked at Mom and tried thinking something nice about her, but it happened again, and the second time, the thoughts were so vivid, it felt like I was doing them just thinking them. My conscience awoke.

"Are you into this?" it asked.

Intent. Intention. Intentionality. Intentar. In Spanish, "to try."

Our desires can, at times, manifest as thoughts. Did I wanna do these things?

A snippet from catechism: the nuns had taught us you don't always sin with your hands. Sometimes, a good imagination's all you need to go to hell. Hell had always been a joke to me. That joke didn't seem funny anymore.

I dried the last plate Mom handed me and left the kitchen in a hurry; I needed to be around family members I wasn't mentally sodomizing. In the family room, I saw Libertad and Vincie watching a movie. I ducked in there and joined them.

"What's on?" I asked.

"The edited-for-TV version of *Witness*," answered Libertad.

Vincie looked bored, but Libertad was happy. She'd gone through a brief Amish phase, and during it, she'd gotten bitter that we weren't German. I remembered she'd quit wearing her normal clothes and had dressed in long Pilgrim skirts and costume bonnets for about a year and a half.

The Amish, now there's a holy people. Maybe because of my wantonness and wicked, worldly lifestyle, I'd made my brain susceptible to that sicko vision. Maybe I needed clothes without buttons and a wimple to cover my hair in order to set me back on the straight and narrow.

I glanced from the undercover masquerade onscreen—*Witness* is about a detective posing as a simple farmer—to Libertad, then to Vincie. They were sitting side by side on one of the sectionals. They were getting big. They were going to be starting seventh grade next year. I pictured myself wrapping my fingers around their throats and squeezing the life out of them. "You want to have sex with their dead bodies," popped into my head.

I could not believe my bad luck. Here were more bad thoughts, and they were spreading to other people, contaminating my reflections. I mentally chanted, "I'm sorry; I love them. I'm sorry; I love them. I'm sorry; I love them."

I rose and went to my bedroom and hid there. I had to avoid my family. All of them. I didn't want to keep killing them or molesting them, even if it was just all in my head.

At dinner, Mom came and knocked on my door and I came out only because I didn't want to draw any suspicion to myself. I went and sat at the table beside Dad like I always did and served myself some green beans and a tortilla and on second thought, an unappetizing pork chop. I rarely ate meat, but maybe I was becoming psycho cause I was iron deficient or something.

I sliced my cutlet into strips and placed one in my mouth. It tasted dry. Dad's chewing sounded loud. I turned to look at him. His jaw moved, grinding his food, and I got this image of myself jacking him off, biting off his penis, and swallowing it whole like those reptiles who don't have gag reflexes and swallow things big as human heads.

I snapped my head away from Dad and fought the urge to cry. I shoveled green beans into my mouth and guzzled my glass of fruit punch.

"I'm done," I mumbled and flew back to my room.

Panting, I ripped my Bible down off its shelf. I combed through it for hours, hunting for any and all passages about demon possession.

Sunday mornings, I usually slept in. The Sunday morning after my subconscious first raped me, I woke up early. And shaking. I didn't want any more of yesterday's disgusting ideas.

In slow-mo, I opened my eyes. I turned my head to look out the window. Three white birches. Dad had planted them on a knoll that gently swelled out of our lawn. The trees stood statue still. The usual breeze wasn't rustling their leaves.

I remained motionless, waiting. Finally, I lifted my hand, examined it. I'd never had tremors before, but now, little jolts of something electrified my muscles. At least there weren't any of those gross thoughts yet. Maybe it was through.

I pushed the covers off me and climbed out of bed, sliding into my house slippers, creeping down the dark hall to the family room. Sweat turned my hands into prunes. I held my palms up to my mouth and blew on them and blew on my fingertips, too.

Dad looked up from the paper. "You're up early."

"Yeah."

I walked past him, through the family room, to the kitchen table. I poured myself a bowl of Lucky Charms and ate. I made myself watch my family. They looked plain as plain could be, doing the stuff families across America were probably doing with their Sunday mornings, too. Mom was behind me at the kitchen counter, fixing her second or third cup of coffee. Dad was sitting in his armchair in his robe, half done with the editorial page of the *Times*. Libertad and Vincie were watching Nickelodeon.

I relaxed and swallowed. I thought, "This is my family. I love them."

I braced myself for nasty thoughts. None came. Maybe it really was over.

Mom said, "Desiree."

I looked at her. She was stirring sugar into her coffee.

"Take out the trash." Mom pulled out her spoon, licked it, and pointed at a knotted plastic sack by her feet.

I nodded and smiled, I couldn't help it; it felt almost euphoric to have my mind back under my control. I went and scooped up the garbage bag and carried it outside, along the concrete path past the roses, across the slab where Mom's Subaru was parked. Libertad's decapitated head invaded the calm. It jostled among the things in the white bag, her raw fibers blending with bacon grease, her blood leaking onto rotten banana peels.

I reached the trashcan pushed against our stucco garage and steadied my shaking hands. I heaved the garbage in and even though I knew it couldn't have been, I untied the knot and took a quick peek just to verify that my sister's head wasn't really hidden inside.

Psycho. Mad girl. Fiend. I was fucking crazy.

I was checking the trash for amputations. Decapitations. I was having heart and chest palpitations. My ribcage pounded like a buffalo stampede through the high plains. Where were the high plains exactly? I had high blood pressure. Did that mean I was excited? Eager? An eager beaver? Eager beaver with a fucking meat cleaver! Why was I rhyming? Rye, Rye, Rye, Rye syndrome.

Tears stung my eyes and clouded my vision. This wasn't how my summer was supposed to be going. I was supposed to be washing my face till it chapped, disinfecting my furniture with ammonia, tapping things and knocking on doorframes with abandon. Instead, I was finally having the big freak out. I was going nuttier than a tin of Planters.

Skirting the garage door, I remembered the hardware Dad stored at his tool bench for his home improvement projects. He had some long metal stakes he used in the yard sometimes. He pounded them into the dirt with a hammer and made sounds like a blacksmith pounding an anvil in his forge. I contemplated hammering one of Dad's stakes through my eye socket, piercing the front part of my brain, giving myself a homemade lobotomy.

A panicky chill cut through me. I sprinted the rest of the way to the front door and hurried back to my room and burrowed back under the covers. My breathing was out of control; it was bordering on hyperventilation.

In and out slowly. In and out slowly. In and out slowly.

My breath slowed down to normal puffs, and I worked on refocusing my mental energy. Using a meditation technique I'd learned in Drama, I drained my body of tension, imagined it leaking like sand through fingers, out my hands, toes, and the top of my head. With my body relaxed, I forced myself to imagine innocent, gentle things.

Deer. Rabbits. Big-eyed squirrels holding humongous acorns.

An urge invaded my pastoral wonderland. It arrived yawn-like, sneeze-like, welling up from a reptilian place inside me. The sensation itched fuzzy, ticklish, and tight, a wool sweater you've gotta pull over your head and get rid of, toss on the floor in a jumbled heap to be forgotten and stepped on. Stepped on.

I had to bleat. I didn't want to, but I had to. I had to make the sound of certain fuzzy animals I'd been thinking about.

Tension held my muscles hostage again. I folded my arms across my chest. I hopped out of bed and began pacing like an expectant father who can hear his wife shrieking in the delivery room. I went back and forth from my closet to my window, wearing a thin path into the carpet. I would not bleat, I would not bleat, I would not bleat. Humming the tune of "Baa, Baa Black Sheep," I tried to distract myself.

I halted dead in my tracks and "Baaaa!" flew out of me. I clamped my hand over my mouth to catch it. The sound escaped and echoed, as if bending off the walls of a small cedar barn.

Mom went to the library to get a fresh cache of summer reading material. I joined her.

I stood in line behind her, watching her check out trashy novels, Collins, Krantz, and Steel embossed on their spines. With her loot deactivated and ready to pass through the alarm, Mom scooped it up and carried it to the exit to wait for me.

"I wish I could be as carefree as Mommy and read pulp," my thoughts began. "Pulp, pulp. Sounds like pulpo. 'Pulpo' means 'octopus' in Spanish. Octopus. Pussy. Pussy eating—"

"Card?"

I looked at the librarian with relief. The urge to say something naughty had begun building in my throat and her interruption had squashed it. I handed her my card. She scanned it with her zapper and began scanning my books.

"*The Ego and the Id*," she read. "Are you writing a report?"

"Uh-huh," I lied.

She scanned *Understanding Freud*. "Intro to Psych?"

I nodded. My body didn't want me to lie. My elbow twitched, up and out.

We got a dog when I was eleven. We saved her from the pound, but she wasn't the kind of dog you normally find there. She was a purebred Yorkshire Terrier, a proper British "dogue." As I sat on a patio bench, trying to think of a good name for her, Dad had watered his bonsais in the backyard.

"What about 'Cleopatra'?" I said. "Or 'Nefertiti'?"

A few feet away from me, my Yorkie had growled at nothing. Or maybe it was a ghost. She spun and chased her stubby tail in tight circles and I wondered how she could do that so fast without falling over. All of a sudden, she quit her circles and took off sprinting in a dangerously straight line. Her head smacked into one of the patio beams, the blow knocking her off her feet. I half expected her to look like a pug when she got up, but when she rose she still had her same snobbish nose. Upturned.

My Yorkie was a champ. She shook off the pain and trotted from the concrete to the lawn where she began doing donuts like a redneck with a new pickup truck. "Yip, yip, yip..." she barked, high-pitched.

"God!" Dad boomed. "That's a neurotic animal!"

The dog quit her workout to stare at a limp garden hose. She sensed innate evil dwelling within it: It was her enemy. To scare the hose, the Yorkie made a vicious, gut driven, unfeminine sound. This was not a noise I thought terriers to be capable of. It was a possum with rabies on the warpath type of sound.

Dad said, "Geez! Talk about Linda Blair! Why don't you call her Linda Blair?"

I glared at him. I hadn't thought it was funny he was comparing my teacup of a pet to the thing that spit up pea soup in *The Exorcist*. Salomé was what I wound up naming the animal. I had no idea what an omen that was, to name my pet for the girl who'd asked for the head of John the Baptist. At that age, I also had only a nebulous notion that Dad was accusing my Yorkie of something bad with that clinical-sounding term, "neurotic." I knew that it had something to do with nerves, but now, six years later, sitting on my carpet with *Understanding Freud* in my lap, Dad's assessment clicked: Salome was damaged goods. She'd been one hair shy of crazy queen bee bitch.

"Focus," my survival instinct reminded me. "You have to fix yourself right now. Forget about that dog. She ran away anyways."

Obeying my instincts, I concentrated on the task at hand. I'd been reading for several hours already in preparation for my own psychoanalysis and armed myself with the fundamental theories of the discipline. As I understood it, I needed to draw into consciousness buried thoughts and feelings. Being neurotic, I tended to repress. This afternoon I was going to have to unleash all my pent-up bullshit, and I prayed my borrowed books could guide me to the light and cut out the middleman.

I cleared my throat and tugged my right earlobe and then the left to even things up. I closed *Understanding Freud* and set it on top of a pile of tomes I'd already skimmed. I reached for a virgin text. The dull afternoon sun filtered in through my window, making my room feel static, matted in a way that usually bothered me. I didn't have time, though, to contemplate what kind of sunlight depressed me. I had to jot my observations in my notebook.

"A) Polymorphously perverse...," I scribbled. I wrote for two pages, using the concept to explain how come I kept having so many sexual and violent thoughts.

"B) I am in an oral, an anal, and a phallic stage..."

"C) I fixate sexually on my mother and my father. I have both an Oedipal and Electra complex..."

I wanted to emerge from my psychosexual drama so bad I could taste it, but according to my guidebooks, I had my work cut out for me. I had to—

Wait.

Freud didn't make sense. First, he'd said that to cure myself I'd have to draw out my hidden desires and face them. Then, he did a total about face, saying we all have incestuous, serial killer thoughts and that we have to learn how not to act on them, to sublimate them.

I didn't want to act on mine. That was the last thing I wanted to do. What I wanted was to *not have the thoughts*. And really, now that I thought about it, what difference did it make if I drew them out? How was that confronting the thoughts? Didn't I confront them every time they happened? Wasn't that the problem? That I was confronting them all day long? All the time?

Pressed for time, I set aside my confusion. I realized that head shrinking was a discipline that also involved a certain measure of faith. I found some and kept on trucking. Night fell and with it, I prayed I'd absorbed enough knowledge to go into battle well armed.

Like a girl preparing to have demons cast out, I leaned back so that my body, from my head to my tail, was flattened against the bedroom floor. The soles of my feet were planted firmly to the ground, my knees arched, my legs apart. I folded my hands and rested them on my stomach. I took a deep breath.

Out loud, I started, "I think about killing Mom. I think about killing Dad. I think about cutting people up. I think about eating them. I..." and I admitted and I admitted and I admitted till I'd squeezed out every single bad thought I could remember. Purged, the words hung in the air around me. I couldn't see them, but they were there. I felt safe. Cleaner.

I shuffled to my knees, they cracked, and I rose and stretched and walked out of my room, across my dark house, to the empty kitchen. Alone, standing at the counter, I ate a Gandhiesque meal: a glass of water and a piece of pita. I felt too exhausted for real food. I set my glass in the sink and brushed a few crumbs off the counter and into the trash and walked back to my unmade bed and climbed in. I dozed off quickly but not before hoping that in the morning, this feeling of purity wouldn't be gone.

By lunchtime the next day, the ugliness had returned. I smeared peanut butter onto a slice of bread and thought of jamming the knife I was using into Libertad's ear, into her brain.

I looked at the kitchen walls and the yellow fridge and microwave and felt them closing in around me. Claustrophobia. I wanted a brain transplant. Freud had failed me.

Maybe I was a human monster. Maybe, at heart, I was that rarest breed, the female serial killer. Ed Gein, he and I were birds of a feather. He killed people and gutted them like deer and he grave-robbed and made a nipple/vagina suit out of his neighbors and he was obsessed with his mother. *Psycho* and *Silence of the Lambs* were loosely based on him.

Maybe I really wanted to do all this sick shit, just like the books said. The more I probed to get at the root of what was causing my morbid thoughts, the worse they got. Within two short weeks, it was knives slitting every throat I saw. A hundred bloodlettings. Green, brown and blue colored eyeballs hanging by bright, red meat strings. Salad forks rammed up anonymous rectums.

Sigmund Freud couldn't have been right, though, that I wanted to do this shit. How could true desires terrify me shitless, set off a million silent alarms, make my conscience go haywire? I wanted to pay someone to cut off my arms and legs so that I could rest assured I'd do no evil. I made sure not to stand too close to my family. I avoided my friends. I avoided animals. Watching TV. Being awake. Thought.

Buddhism seemed like the trick. I tried emptying my mind. My imagination relented. It would not be stifled but I needed a crutch to help me withstand the onslaught. A compulsion. Compulsions. A slew of new ones:

— Keep a distance from all living creatures while chanting mental mantras: "I shall not covet. I shall not covet. Forgive me, Lord Jesus in heaven, you know the evil that I am."

— Unimagine the imagined. Push the rewind button on the VCR while the tape's still playing and watch everything disappear.

— Apologize to victims, albeit silently, in your head: "I'm so sorry. I will burn in hell for killing you."

Ted Bundy. Jeffrey Dahmer. John Wayne Gacy. Desiree Garcia.

I used to joke I was a Satanist. Now I prayed so much to Jesus and the saints that I was worse than the nuns from school. At least it comforted me to know that the holiest of people had been plagued by bad thoughts, too. Saint Teresa of Lisieux. Ignatius of Loyola. I knew they were good, and I was evil, and that even comparing my suffering to theirs was a sin.

I knelt more than I stood.

I wanted to be nailed to a cross.

My mind became a medieval prison. A monastery. I stopped playing games with my Mexican rosary and started using it.

Salt and Pepper

That August, Mom took me to Mexico with her.

Sodom and Gomorrah still defined the landscape of my mind so as we boarded our flight, I forced myself to think happy thoughts about my fellow passengers, especially the pilots. I feared if I didn't make myself do this, I'd start imagining myself snapping and committing some awful misdeed, like me strangling stewardesses and hijacking our airplane and crashing it into a six-hundred-year-old Aztec pyramid, a modern day human sacrifice that'd make it onto the world news.

As I struggled to spin compliments like, "Wow, that steward has really nice highlights," my right shoulder betrayed my inner turmoil. It flinched back like I was an angler reeling in a stubborn ten-pound bass. Before it whapped the big haired lady behind me with the tattooed eyebrows, I grabbed my hand and twisted it.

I turned to face the woman. "Desculpas[62]?" I begged.

Ugly eyebrows was not very forgiving. She nodded curtly.

Mom found us our seats, and she settled into the one by the window. I eased in beside her and strapped on my seatbelt, pulling it tight. I relaxed my elbows on the armrests and inhaled, holding the air in my lungs. Our ascent began. An exhale and my foot kicked out, tapped by an invisible hammer testing my reflexes. My hand pressed my knee down but the energy escaped through my heel. It tapped, tapped, tapped, and I turned and yanked a pocket book of verse from my bag, hoping that some poetry would calm me down.

Music soothes the savage beast.

Edna St. Vincent Millay. A graduation gift.

Just as I'd begun to lull myself into thinking that my limbs were back under my control, I realized yes, my slim volume was moving. I was moving it. My right hand was flicking it back.

I looked at Mom to see if she'd noticed. The back of her head. White hairs mixed in with black ones. She was gazing out the window.

I shut my book and let it slide into my lap. I shut my eyes.

Mom woke me up. A stewardess was standing beside me with lunch. I opened my eyes long enough to choke down a bite of corn and sip some orange juice and I felt Mom's eyes on me.

"Are you feeling okay?" she asked.

I nodded.

She reached out and touched my forehead. I wasn't running a fever. Mom pulled her hand away and rested her head back against her seat cushion and shut her eyes.

I shut my eyes again, too, pretending to nap. Really, I was panicking. I wasn't neurotic. I wasn't touched by God. Or the devil. I was insane. True insane. Snake sounding nuts. Hissss. With an 's.' Pssssychosis. Sssschizophrenia. P and ssss. Ssss and p. Ssssal y pimienta. Ssssalt and

---

62   Forgive me?

pepper. Pepper. Pass the pepper. Please pass the pepper.

Quick and quiet and imperceptibly, I mouthed, "Pass the pepper." I had to. There was the proof. S and P.

The plane landed. We were given the go ahead to disembark.

Following the rest of the lemmings, me and Mom trailed behind the carry-on toting masses, back up the center aisle. Salt and pepper, salt and pepper, salt and pepper...

Mom and Tia Fe stood in the kitchen, chatting. I was helping them get dinner ready and was aware that Mom had been making comments directed at me and Tia had winked at me at least once but if some ski-masked guy held a gun to my head and said, "Tell me what they were talking about or I'll shoot you," I'd have lost my life.

The entire time I'd been with them, I'd been obsessing on acting like a Saint Bernard. I wanted to lick Mom. I wanted to lick Tia. I wanted to stick my tongue out and press it to everyone and everything.

Lick.

Was I regressing to an oral phase? Oh, fuck it. Who knew? What I did know was that every muscle and joint in my body was tensed and ready to rip apart or snap. I was on the rack, fully taut, and some part of my brain thought this was funny. Lick. It yanked the ropes tighter.

"This is the last straw," I thought. The thought felt wrong. I'd thought it incorrectly. I re-thought the words to get their rhythm right.

"This is the last straw."

"This is the last straw."

"This is the last straw."

I could now move on to my next thought.

Licking people was abominable. But I wanted to do it so bad. Had to. I had to get rid of this feeling.

"I'm going to go change my clothes," I mumbled.

I got up from the table and hiked up the cramped spiral staircase that connected the kitchen to the second story. Hurrying into the room me and Mom were sharing, I shut the door behind me and locked it and took off my t-shirt and jeans. In my bra and cotton underwear, I sat on Chata's bed. Squeak. I lifted my wrist about four inches from my eyes, looked at it. My favorite bone, I wasn't sure what it was called, maybe it was just a shapely part of my radius, curved sexy. At the top of it, there was a tiny mole.

I licked the spot. Then, I bit it, as hard as I could. I hadn't been expecting the bite. The chomp. I unclamped me teeth and held my wrist in front of my eyes to behold the impression. A dentist could have used the marks to fit me with dentures. I sniffed the spit. It stank. Disgusting.

I changed into a skirt and blouse and clogs and walked back to the first floor using the main staircase. My legs wobbled. I heard the doorbell ring.

Maybe if I did a good deed, a kind deed, a normal deed, like answering the rings, it'd cancel out the bizarro thing I'd just done. I headed to the foyer to let in whoever was buzzing. Stepping through the archway, I saw Nito standing by the fountain, by the ferns, holding a dozen red roses ready to but not quite bursting into full bloom. He saw me and held the bouquet out.

"Para ti[63]," he said.

I clenched my teeth. "Gracias."

I walked over to him, ripped the bouquet out of his hand, and stomped to the kitchen. The swinging door swished behind as I entered and Mom and Tia looked up, teary-eyed from onion dicing. I pointed towards the foyer.

"Did you know he was coming?" I asked Tia.

She smiled. "I told you we were going to have a special visitor," she answered.

---

63   For you

156

Mom picked up the flowers I'd dropped on the table. "Very pretty," she said.

"Hmph."

I tried to take refuge in the kitchen till it was time to eat, but Mom expelled me.

"Go talk to Nito!" she ordered.

I pouted and left the kitchen and wandered into the living room. Nito was sitting on the love seat.

"I need to talk to you," he said.

I nodded and let him lead me to a weather worn equipal out in the backyard. Nito sat. I remained standing.

"I love you," he said.

"You love me?" I echoed. "People who love other people don't cast spells on them!"

Nito acted aghast. "That wasn't a spell!"

"Yes it was! You sent that weird package with that poem and that wheel! You sent that voodoo, you liar. I'm offended. I'm offended that anyone would think that they could just cast a spell on me and they could make me into a zombie."

"You don't love me?"

I folded my arms. "No. I hate you."

A dark curtain fell over Nito's face.

"Very well," he said. "Very well, Desiree."

Nito rose, limped across the tiled patio, through the open glass door, and, knock on wood, out of this girl's life for good.

(2)

Carnie

Four years later, during my last year of college, Rae, my girlfriend, crouched beside me on our bedroom floor. Mortified and helpless, she stared at me, all crumpled against the wall. She'd been trying hard to comfort me, but her magic wasn't working this time.

"There're no lice in your hair," she said. "I promise. I've already checked it twice... It's just your OCD."

I huddled, wedged into the tight space between my nightstand and the corner, a drop of clear snot dangling from the tip of my nose.

"I know," I bawled, "but could you just check it one more time? Please? The lady on the bus next to me kept scratching her head and then mine started to itch."

Rae sighed and reached back into my hair and she began the long process of combing through it, strand by strand, the third time around. Only someone who loves you no matter what would do that, be your chimp. Getting my head checked for bugs means somebody loves me, and I met my somebody, Rae, when I was going to school at Berkeley. That's where I went after St. Mike's. Now I know Berkeley's got a fancy reputation but I don't fool myself. I got in because of affirmative action. Let in the Mexicans! Fill the quotas. They'll give the crackers a run for their money!

I didn't. I couldn't even tell you what it was like going there; I don't recollect much. I spent four years staggering around that leviathan campus, dizzy, purple from holding so much in. On bad days, I forgot to breathe. Junior year, I bit a page out of Machiavelli's The Prince and instead of jumping out of my sixth story window, I made an appointment to see someone. A psychiatrist. Dr. Rose. On her leather office couch, I let the deluge come pouring out of me.

"I think about killing people...I think about stabbing people... I think about raping people...I think about such sick things," I confessed, sobbing into a tattered Kleenex that was five seconds from disintegrating.

Dr. Rose stood, and I genuinely thought she was coming over to me to hug me. Instead, she waddled her fat ass over to a metal file cabinet, opened a drawer, and rooted around. She pulled out a pamphlet, brought it back to me, and foisted it onto my lap.

I glanced at the cover. *Obsessive-Compulsive Disorder.*

"Read it," she commanded.

I flipped through the first several pages. The pamphlet's "Typical OCD" vignettes seemed benign, cake compared with what I was suffering. A businessman whose hands bled from a little too much washing. A third grade girl who was late to school cause of excessive light-switch checking. A housewife who had to count all the electrical outlets in a room before she could sit down comfortably.

There weren't any descriptions of Chicana dykes worrying they might become serial killers.

"This isn't me," I thought and turned to the last page. A neo-impressionist rendering of Howard Hughes accompanied the section entitled, "Severe Cases." I stared at the famous aviator now depicted as a googly-eyed fruitcake. A long scraggly beard and unkempt hair tumbled past his chin and shoulders and his claws curved into talons, like the Asian guy with the longest nails in history from the *Guinness Book of World Records*. Track marks dotted Hughes' skinny arms. Okay. That was enough.

I slammed the pamphlet shut and looked up at Dr. Rose.

"What do you think?" she'd asked.

"I don't know," I said, hesitating. I started playing with my hair. "There's more. Can I tell you more?"

"Go ahead."

"Sometimes... I move."

"You move?"

"Yeah. I move. Like, let's say, my leg will kick out."

"Show me."

"I can't. It just happens. A certain way."

Dr. Rose stared at me. It made me very uncomfortable.

"What else?"

"I want to cuss," I admitted.

"Everybody cusses."

"I know. But this is different. The other day, I almost screamed 'Cunt!' at the top of my lungs. I was just waiting in line for a bagel."

"Were you mad about something?"

"No! It just came out of nowhere."

"Did you say it?"

"Not exactly."

"What do you mean?"

"The word kept repeating in my head and it finally stopped when I whispered the 'cu' sound to myself."

Dr. Rose leaned back in her chair. She wore a blank expression. "Desiree, that's not OCD," she explained. "You have two disorders. The second one..."

I listened but then OCD rang the doorbell. I let it in.

"Never trust doctors," it advised. "They make mistakes. Leave the field of diagnosis open. Do it yourself." OCD turned and left.

I nodded at everything Dr. Rose explained about my illnesses and at the end, I assured her, "I'll call you for another appointment." Lies.

Walking home, I'd thought to myself, "I have schizophrenia, I have schizophrenia, I have schizophrenia," in multiples of three.

I confided in no one about my dual diagnoses and since I basically become a hermit, there was no one to tell anyways. The only person I eventually mentioned anything to was Rae. We'd done, like, the whole lesbian cliché thing, met in a bar, and then, you know the punch line:

What do two lesbians do on a second date?

Rent a U-Haul!

Me and my boi shacked up lickety-split, and in the beginning, it was great because we scored a cheap apartment in North Oakland, on Telegraph Avenue, right across the street from the Lady of Shalott feminist bookstore, and we had kinky sex all the time with huge dildos but as to be expected, the honeymoon ended.

I let Rae catch me sitting on the toilet, my index finger pressed to my wrist, my eyes glued to the minute hand on my watch, when she came home from work one night.

"What're you doing?" she asked. She started unbuttoning the shirt part of her security guard uniform.

"Taking my pulse."

She laughed, "Are you a hypochondriac?"

"No. But a shrink once told me I have OCD."

"Do you?"

"Prob'ly."

Rae could've run away when I broke the news to her so nonchalant. But she stayed. I believe she did because of how she was raised, by her grandpa in his traveling carnival, Pooler's Amusements. The man was a talented, one-armed electrician who got her used to the sideshow climate, midways, the ballyhoo. My odd behavior was normal compared with the real-live circuses she'd grown up in, and Rae's been so understanding she's even allowed me to teach her to accommodate my illness. At one point, I had my baby trained so good Rae could sense if I was in an odd or even mood and repeat a wrong phrase just right till it pleased me. She gave me oodles of reassurance and did lots of checking for me, but, recently, she's begun cutting back.

It's 'cause Rae's trying to help me.

First, she convinced me to quit stripping. It's not as ironic a career for a Berkeley grad with an obsessive-compulsive disability as one might think. In fact, there's a plethora of unstable, well-educated strippers in the Bay Area. I liked the work very much. My schedule was flexible, leaving me with plenty of time to stay home and do rituals, and where I worked, at The Steamin' Delta, our boss encouraged us to rub down the pole with copious amounts of disinfectant before grinding it. Plus, dancing on stage and for my customers, I didn't have to worry about you-know-what. All I had to do was focus on moving my body to the rhythm of the music and giving guys boners, and the consequent harmony and order of it all subdued my monster.

Still, Rae begged me to stop. And I get why. It wasn't part of the I'm-gonna-save-you-from-sex-work-baby! routine. Rae's not like that, although I do think she lived a little in fear of stripper burnout. She's had stripper girlfriends before. No, what Rae really wanted for me was to get a good job, a job with benefits, a job that provided me with health insurance in case shit happened. She found me one, through the classifieds, at Animo School for Adults, smack dab on the Oakland/Berkeley border, upstairs from the most popular Korean barbecue in town.

Same week I started teaching night school, I thought Rae was going to propose to me.

"I bought you something," she said.

She'd made me dinner, a juicy vegetarian lasagne, no ricotta, steamed vegetables on the side, and was clearing the dishes. I sipped wine with my hand down my pants and pictured Rae whipping out a diamond ring, getting down on one knee.

The table was empty except for our bottle of wine and a vase full of fresh daisies. Rae turned and strode across our small kitchen, to a cabinet by the boiler. She peeked inside. She walked back carrying a pink bag with a flouncy black bow on it, setting the bag down in front of me.

I looked down at Rae's hands as they retreated back to her sides. They're gnarled from years of construction work and house cleaning and smeary tattoos start at her wrists while farther up, clearer, newer ones crawl all the way to her shoulders. My favorite she got to honor the memory of her grandpa, Clyde Delmore Pooler, after he died. It's a gaudy Ferris wheel spinning on her bicep.

When Rae first showed me the tattoo, she slapped the ride and said, "I can take one of these apart and put it back together again with my eyes shut. Learned how to when I was knee high to a junebug."

I traced the ink with my fingers and asked, "Know what?"

Rae shook her head and grinned.

I admired the gap between her two front teeth and tapped the top gondola on her Ferris wheel and said, "I imagine me and you making out, stuck right here forever, no one able to rescue us."

Rae gets me pure and simple, my frustrations with the loop tape that is my thought process, the boiling pot that is my body. She feels my frustrations because she got a mix-up, too; she's not really a girl. Like, she's got a pussy covered with thick hair and she's got a full rack, but she's really a guy trapped in a gold mine of a stripper's body. As a he-she, Rae knows what it's like to feel bananas. Just like I'm chaotic neurotransmitters imprisoned by flesh and bone, she's masculinity poured into a body that curves like a Coke bottle.

"Oh, Rae," I breathed, touching the black bow. "You shouldn't have."

"Go on," she urged. "Open it."

I untied the bow and set it aside. I plunged my hand into the bag and felt a book cover. I pulled out *Taming Your OCD: A Self-Help Workbook and Guide*.

Coming from anybody else, this would've been a slap in the face. Coming from Rae, I loved it. I looked into her brown eyes.

"You want me to get better, don't you?" I asked softly.

"Did June Carter want Johnny Cash to?"

"That's sweet," I said.

"I'll do the dishes. Why don't you go read?"

I nodded.

I picked up my book, carried it with me to the pink-carpeted living room, and lay down on the plaid couch across from the TV. It's a four-legged orphan I rescued from the curb where a neighbor abandoned it along with his Christmas tree. That might be appropriate treatment for a useless cadaver but not trash. People underestimate trash, forgetting about how much life-potential things possess, and our living room demonstrates this axiom.

Take our coffee table, for example. It's a lavender piece of kitsch we bought off a crackhead at the flea market for three bucks. If we hadn't bought it, who knows where it would've wound up. Our Art Linkletter barcalounger is the same story, a Goodwill score, and the blaxploitation movie posters I tacked up on our walls are relics I caught my landlord trying to throw away.

John Willie postcards of bondage girls are the main decor hanging in our living room. I happened upon a shoebox at a yard sale and they were inside. I haggled with their seller over the cost.

"Fine," he finally said in order to get rid of me. "Take 'em for a quarter."

I did. Now, in tiny frames, damsels in distress dot my walls.

Hogtied girls comfort me, and I wonder about the girls in the photos sometimes, how some of them are probably great-grandmas now or are maybe deceased, and how back in the day, for extra cash to buy heroin or feed the kids or pay the rent, the ladies dressed up in bullet bras and black girdles and stockings and let people tie them up.

I stared at the postcard of the girl with Marcel-waved hair. She was gagged, restrained. From how the ropes looked, you could tell she was resisting a little, for show. Marcel Waves' picture in particular makes me feel safe. I think it's because rope burn makes me feel safe. I like being tied up. I let Rae do it to me whenever she feels like. I let her whip me with her belt, too. It's sexy and we have a safe word for when it gets too intense.

Pickles.

I looked away from Marcel Waves and opened my book. Taking a deep breath, I let my eyes slide across its table of contents. The chapters had promising, un-Freudian sounding titles like "Becoming Your Own Therapist" and "Cognitive Behavioral Therapy: A Proven Treatment Method." Instead of reading through the workbook in sequence, I skipped around, looking through the vignettes that appeared every couple of pages in italics. I found it about half an hour in, a description of a high school girl who was in her bedroom one afternoon, doing her homework, who out of the blue started to wonder, "What if I walked into the kitchen right now, pulled a knife out of the drawer and stabbed my whole family with it?"

There I lived and breathed in the pages of a self-help workbook. My hands started to tremble.

"Rae!" I yelped.

She couldn't hear me over the cacophony of dishwashing.

I flipped to Chapter 20, "Related Disorders."

Trichotillomania, nicknamed "trick": the pulling out of one's own hair.

Body Dysmorphic Disorder, BDD: seeing oneself as deformed when one clearly isn't.

Tourette's: tics, semi-voluntary, hard to control sounds and movements that besiege you constantly. Common ones? Hair twirling, eye blinking. Sniffing. Jerking arms, jerking neck. Twitching. Uncommon ones? Coprolalia. In Greek, fecal talk. Compulsive swearing, only 15% of Touretters have it. And they don't always give in. Some Touretters find creative ways of satisfying it. Repeating the words up in the old noggin. Making barely audible sounds to scratch the dirty word itch.

I clapped the book shut, and clutching it to my chest, got up and walked to the kitchen. I stood by the refrigerator.

"Rae," I said. I was crying, stupid as it sounds, tears of joy.

She hollered, "You scared me! Don't sneak up on me like that!" Slowly, Rae turned to face me. Her wet fingertips rained water onto the kitchen tile. Her smile dropped. Mine didn't.

"What's wrong?" she asked.

I grinned. "Rae. I have Tourette's."

Extra Terrestrial

I replaced Animo's most popular ESL teacher, el profesor Alvaro, and my boss, Principal Shields, tried putting a scare into me before letting me take his position.

"They loved Alvaro," he warned me grimly. "They might eat you alive."

"I'm up to the challenge," I answered. I signed my name on the dotted line, good as swearing a blood oath.

Mustafa, the Afghani security guard who patrols Animo, walked me up to my classroom on my first night.

"You want to know why Alvaro leave?" he asked.

"Why?"

"He fired! Evedy Friday night was fiesta! The estudents bring up coolers of esodas and emusic and edance and profesor Alvaro," he pronounced well en Español, "sit at his desk and watch. Efood lady cam and sell tamales and tacos and tortas and Alvaro, he take part of the cut! He erunning enight club, enot eschool!"

I raised my eyebrows. What kind of racket was I getting myself into? I feared I was being fed to a pack of partying piranhas but as I stood, facing my students for the first time, I realized Principal Shields and Mustafa had pegged them all wrong. They all looked like my mom more or less. Harmless. Plus, they were adaptable. They might've loved Alvaro once but they got over him quick. They were going to fall in love with anyone willing to teach them English.

Two weeks in, compliments showered me. Principal Shields was impressed. "Chee teach us much more than Profesor Alvaro!" I overhead Lupe Diaz tell Mustafa. "Chee eez a fun, happy teacher!"

Advice from my workbook made adjusting to my new job easier, too. I stood at the blackboard, intrusive images flooding my consciousness, but like *Taming Your OCD* instructed, I let them enter; I put up no fight. This yanked the rug out from under them. The suckers melted into so much background. It was weird. All I had to do was welcome the sickness and it became a teddy bear, no longer a slimy-toothed grizzly. The urges didn't disappear quite the same way, but once I got into the groove of lessons, I realized they usually quieted of their own accord. Demonstrating verbs on my hands and knees, pretending to be an exotic noun, I'm usually too busy to be interrupted by tics.

ESL tends to be a gender-skewed affair, and most of my students are women. Some are stay-at-home moms who want to learn English in their spare time, but others are the backbones of entire black market industries, captains of major under-the-table enterprises. Take Lupe Diaz, for example. She's a baker whose cakes are in demand for everything from Bat Mitzvahs to quinceañaras. Sylvia Mendez cleans houses naked all over the bay. Julia Juarez is becoming a millionaire selling Herbalife.

I pity my few male students. They're swimming in a sea of estrogen.

In level one, I've got a teenaged boy who should be attending public high school. The registrar claims they're all full though, so he's stuck till next fall with me and the clucking comadres[64]. In level two, I've got a retired janitor and his son. The father's got a silver moustache and goes by the distinguished-sounding "Don Chencho." The kid seems like riff-raff, a snot-nosed cholo.

Recently, a newbie hopped into Level Two on crutches. His name was printed on the night's roster but when I called it during roll, he corrected me.

"Not Luis Guzman," he said. "El Tecolote."

Sara Martinez giggled. Lupe Diaz's jaw dropped. Julia Juarez's eyes twinkled. I cocked one eyebrow at the guy. He was asking to be called The Owl.

"El Tecolote?"

"Jes," he grinned.

I got nervous. Oh shit. A major urge to hoot. My hands got sweaty. I balled up my fists. I would not hoot.

"Can I call you E.T.?" I blurted out.

"Jes. E.T. eez okay."

"Okay, E.T... E.T. it is."

Beside his name, in pencil, I wrote, "Lunatic."

I went to dinner with Animo's math teacher, Artie, before work. We sat under a donkey piñata at La Fiesta, waiting for our waitress to bring us our burritos. Artie drank a beer. I sipped water.

"Have you got that El Tecolote in any of your classes?" Artie asked me.

"Yeah! I call him E.T."

Artie laughed and salsa spilled off his chip and splattered onto the front of his Hawaiian shirt. The guy's an aging surfer, a manic Hispanic

---

64   Formally, godmother; informally, a lady-pal

from back in the day who really wants to retire to Oahu when he's done teaching. He's almost there. He's only got, like, two years left to go. I watched him wet a paper napkin and wipe the stain.

"E.T.," he laughed one last time. Then his tone changed. "That fucker's such a fraud. You know what the big chisme[65] on him is?"

I shook my head.

"Supposedly he got his legs crushed in a forklifting accident. He claims one of them got torn to shreds and he got himself one of them personal injury ambulance chasers and took his boss to court. He's gotten part of his settlement but he's waiting for an even bigger part of it to come now. Guess how much."

"I don't like guessing." I twirled my hair with both hands. Artie didn't seem to mind. "How much?"

"Two hundred thou."

"Jesus!"

"Yeah. But guess what?"

"What?"

"I know that fucker's full of shit. Ain't nothin' wrong with his legs. I swear to God, I seen him hot-footin' it up Shattuck to catch the bus."

"Serious?"

"Serious. He was carrying his crutches and everything. He was running."

"Man."

"God, I hate assholes like that. They come over here and work the system and they give people like you and me," he gestured at us, "a bad name."

I didn't like Artie's cynicism, but I was too hungry to argue.

"I hate those fuckers," he mumbled and shoved a handful of tortilla chips into his mouth.

---

65   gossip

Despite the mariachi music, I could hear Artie's crunching. It made my toes tic. Bad.

El Tecolote showed up late to class. He looked a little drugged. I paused the lesson.

"Why tardy?" I asked him.

"Heedro-eterapy. Efor mai leg," he answered. "I seat een yacuzzi weet babbles for lon time."

"Heedro-eterapy, heedro-eterapy, heedro-etarpy," I thought. Bingo. Hydrotherapy. I turned around and erased the verb "to be" off the chalkboard and rolled my eyes. Fucking hydrotherapy. I turned back around.

"Okay, E.T. Have a seat."

Because I was running out of ideas, I was in the midst of killing my students with grammar drills. I'd dittoed them to death for two hours and the class was quiet, all the ladies chewing their pens, stumped by my page of irregular verbs. I didn't like the silence. It unnerved me. It made me feel like jerking.

I dismissed class fifteen minutes early. Mustafa came by and poked his head in through the door.

"Everyting alright, ma'am?" he asked.

"Yes. Everything's fine."

I wanted to lick the chalkboard, count cracks in the ceiling, but E.T. was loitering. He had his gimp leg propped up on a chair. He stared at me.

"Can I help you with something?" I asked.

"Jes."

"What?"

I sat down behind my desk, which I never do. I hate it. Usually, it makes me feel bad to sit at it, like "I'm the teacher, I sit here. You're the students, you sit there." The desk creates stratification. In this instance, however, the desk offered protection. I wore it like a fort. It was a big wooden barricade separating me from danger.

E.T. hoisted himself up, propped himself against his crutches and hopped over. He stopped two feet from the desk and watched me pick up a red pen. I began grading papers with it.

"Meece Garcia," he began. "I leeb een a duplex⬚"

"Luis," I interrupted. "Just tell me in Spanish."

He nodded and smiled. In Spanish, he repeated, "Señorita Garcia, I live in a duplex. With my mother. She has diabetes. The building is for sale and my attorney told me it's a good investment; I should buy it. There is one problem, however."

"What?"

"I am not a citizen," he grinned sheepishly. "But if I put the house in a citizen's name, it will be okay. And the citizen can live in the other half. For free." He stared at me.

I wished for Mustafa to poke his head in right then. E.T. had me cornered but I couldn't show him that he was making me angry or nervous.

"Are you saying what I think you're saying?" I asked.

Same stupid grin.

"Uh-uh. No," I answered. "And what you are suggesting is very wrong. On many different levels. I've gotta go."

"Wait!" he cried in English. "Joo meesunderstand me."

"No, I didn't," I said firmly. "I've gotta clean up here and shut out the lights. You need to go."

He looked at me funny. "E.T. is sorry," he said.

"Fine. Goodnight, E.T."

"Goodnight, Meece Garcia," he said and hopped away.

For my twenty-second birthday, Lupe Diaz baked me a cake in the shape of a princess. She wore a pink frosting dress with gold beads on it and a tiara on her blonde head.

"Eez joo," said E.T.

The students looked at him like he was retarded. I ignored him.

"Cut me a piece of her skirt!" I said.

Lupe handed me a big, tasty piece of petticoat and Julia served me flan and gelatin treats the other ladies had brought from home and instead of studying English, we spent the evening singing and doing the limbo under a broomstick.

We were having plenty of fun, but then E.T. got up and hopped to the boom box. He pushed stop. The cumbia[66] ended.

"Aw," people grumbled.

E.T. ignored the whines. "Attention!" he cried. People looked at one another, rolling their eyes. "Attention please!" he cried in English.

People sat at their desks and folded their arms, letting E.T. speak.

He cleared his throat and continued in Spanish, "I have composed an original work in honor of this evening, for the birthday celebration of our teacher. It is a poem entitled 'Poetry.' " E.T. lifted a sheet of lined paper to his face and grew quiet.

"It was at that age...," he read, and he delivered a beautiful poem about the nature of poetry, of it finding you, not you finding it, and it taking you and you realizing that you are none other than poetry itself. "Poetry" is by Pablo Neruda. I took a seminar on his work senior year at Cal. Dad had insisted it was a useless class. Now I could prove to him that it wasn't.

E.T. whispered the poem's final word, "...wind," and the class sat, amazed. Slowly, they began to nod their heads and clap. Nena Rodriguez, who thinks she's very sexy, lifted her cup of atole[67] in the air and cried, "Little did we know we had a poet among us." She brought

---

66   Colombian dance music, heavy on percussion
67   A hot cornstarch-based drink

her cup down and clasped her arms firmly to her sides, intentionally squeezing out more cleavage for the writer.

Lupe shook her head in disgust.

At 9:30, Sylvia took charge of a clean-up crew that wiped away the pachanga in no time, had the space looking like a classroom again within minutes. Lupe scooped my leftover cake into a pink box and gestured for me to join her behind the file cabinets. I went and stood beside her and in her husky voice, Lupe whispered to me in Spanish, "Be careful, Señorita Garcia. El Tecolote knows you are gay."

"He knows I'm gay?" I was astonished.

"Yes. He told Nena Rodriguez that he saw you kissing a woman with big breasts who looked like a man at the flea market on Ashby. Be careful. He told her, 'I am going to change the teacher! She is too pretty to be a lesbian.'"

"Thank you," I whispered to Lupe. On second thought, I added, "Are you okay with it?"

"With what?"

"With me being gay."

Lupe nodded, "Of course. My sister is gay."

I left Animo weighted down with leftover princess cake and gifts. I walked up Telegraph Avenue alone, past the organic foods market and the dentists' offices, and the piercing parlor. The whole time, I felt like I was being watched. I got to my building and took my key out of my pocket and spun around to look over my shoulder. In the bushes beside the Lady of Shalott, I heard leaves rustle and crutches fall, clattering to the ground.

Right To Bear Arms

Oakland First Presbyterian is a brown and white church that looks a bit like a photograph I once saw accompanying an encyclopedia article about the Globe Theatre.

It's got a white face with brown crisscrossing beams over it and little apses poking out here and there. I know for a fact AA holds meetings there because on our way to Jack London Square one night me and Charlie drove past First Presbyterian and clustered outside we saw blacks, whites, Asians, and brown people all being nice to each other. There were rich and poor, greaser and soc, talking pleasantly, sharing cigarettes, sipping coffee from Styrofoam cups. It was Martin Luther King Jr.'s speech manifest.

That's what an AA meeting is all about, sitting at the table of brotherhood, I Have a Dream, and if you see a similar-looking crowd but they've got hepatitis and are dressed a little funkier, don't fear: That's just NA.

Sunday afternoon, I looked at the concrete ground outside First Presbyterian's main entrance. Cigarette butts littered it, evidence, good as fresh dung or rabbit tracks, that the Friends of Bill W. had indeed conducted a recent meeting. I was procrastinating, already half an hour late for the one I'd come to attend, the monthly gathering of Oakland's T.S.O. chapter, the Tourette Syndrome Organization. I'd found the D.C. headquarters' number listed in the resources section of my workbook and on a lark, I'd called them up and gotten the skinny about support group locations and dates and times.

I did one of those deep kneebends I only do when I'm nervous as heck. What was I gonna see in the Round Table Room? Knights? King Arthur? That was the epic-sounding name of the place where a woman named Lorraine who I'd spoken to on the phone had told me to go.

I stared up at the steeple and worried, "What if I don't really have Tourette's? What if I have early onset Parkinson's? I'll die soon if I didn't get proper medical treatment!"

"Stop it!" I hissed at myself and stood up straight and jammed my hands into my coat pockets.

I walked through the church's tall doorway and followed the signs left, down the hall. Standing six feet from the Round Table Room's door, I heard a woman growl, "Nappy niggers!"

I braced myself. I wished for a second I'd taken Rae up on her offer to come with me. Then I walked in alone.

A mixture of kids and adults sat on folding chairs organized into a circle. A podium was pushed into a corner and a table had been collapsed and stacked against a wall to make room for the meeting. I scanned the faces to see if I could make out who I'd heard screaming from the hall.

"May I help you?" a man with glasses and a shiny red nose asked me.

"Yeah. I'm Desiree. I called last week. Someone named Lorraine told me to come here."

"Oh. That's my dwaughter," he explained in a thick New York accent. "Have a seat, deah. I'm Glen. The group maderatuh." After I sat in an empty chair beside a little ginger boy who kept flinging his head back and snorting, Glen said, "Nancy was just finishin' up."

He gave the floor to a wholesome twentysomething with a face like a sitcom star's, plain Jane pretty enough for people to project their own fantasies onto. Glen stared at her, one hand on his knee, the other stroking his spiky, white beard. Glen's glasses glinted. His hair looked windswept. I wondered if the motorcycle helmet beside his chair belonged to him.

I focused on Nancy. Her fingers played with a plastic drinking straw, and she mangled it, twisting it and twisting it and twisting it. Her leg jiggled, too, bouncing up and down, and a woman who looked like an older version of her stroked her hair.

"So, as I was saying," Nancy said, "I was in a crunch and it was close to finals. I had a paper due, and shame on me, tsk, tsk, tsk, I had a coffee drink." Nancy turned to the woman smoothing her hair and looked at her with remorse. She glanced back at the rest of us. "Well, I paid the price. I went to my early childhood development class but I couldn't even stay in my seat 'cause my tics were so out of control so I excused myself to the back of the room where I thought I wouldn't bother anybody and let everything out."

The memory made her widen her eyes, and she laughed. "The professor, well, he called a break and motioned for me to come over to him and he asked me in this very serious voice, 'Are you ill, young lady?' "

Glen and the woman who had to be Nancy's mother laughed.

"I said, 'No. I have Tourette's Syndrome.' He looked at me like he didn't know what I was talking about so I went to his desk and wrote it down for him on a piece of paper and handed it to him. 'It's a neurological disorder,' I explained to him. 'Look it up on the internet.

I'm fine.'"

Glen grinned. "This gal is great!" he gushed.

Nancy put both hands on her knees and pushed forward. "Well, the professor just took the note and put it in his pocket and he put his hands on my shoulders like this," she held hers up and out, "and he looked me in the eye and said, 'You. Are. Not. Well. Is there someone you can call to come get you?'

"I told him, 'I'm fine, but if I'm being too disruptive to the class, I can go.'

" 'Please,' he said. 'Go. You are not well.' "

Glen roared with laughter. "He's the one who's not well! He's the one who's not well, by gosh! What a great story." Glen turned to me. "You should listen to Nancy, uh, Desiree. She's amazin'. She's in City College, gettin' huh AA. The Depahtment of Rehabilitation is payin' fuh huh education and she's got a job as a waitress, too. It can be done," he stressed.

I twirled my hair ferociously and looked at the smug bastard. He was head over heels in love with Nancy. Or at least infatuated by her perky twins.

"Thanks," I offered. "But I'm already graduated."

"From whe'?"

"Berkeley."

Silence.

"So what is it that brings ya heah, Desiree?" Glen asked.

All eyes on me.

I stopped twirling. "I think I have Tourette's," I said plainly.

An Asian teenager with pink hair echoed, "I think I have Tourette's."

"What do you do?" Glen asked me.

"I'm a teacher."

"No. I mean, tics."

Coming to the meeting had been a big step for me but I wasn't sure if I was ready to tell a bunch of strangers what I'd been struggling to hide from the whole wide world since I was eleven.

"Stuff," I teased. Oh, what the hell. I could tell them a little. "Lots of stuff. With my fingers and hands. My head. Stuff. Words. Usually I hold it in."

"It makes you anxious," said Nancy, "huh?"

The pink-haired girl echoed, "...makes you anxious, huh?"

"Uh-huh," I said. "A lot."

Nancy shook her head back and forth. "It's from holding in all your tics. It's best if you just let them out. Believe me."

Duh.

Nancy's eyes widened, and she moaned, "You're a nice nigger!"

Whoa. Okay. Now I knew who I'd heard screaming from the hallway. I looked around the room to gauge the other people's reactions. They acted like this was normal. I heard spitting and turned to see a chunky blonde boy to my right wiping a gob of saliva tenderly from his tired mother's hair.

"I'm sorry, Mom," he apologized. "I love you."

She hugged his husky shoulder. "I know," she said.

"I know," the pink-haired girl echoed.

A cuckoo clock sounded. Nancy. She slapped both her knees and cried, "Thick shit! Shit stick. Shit stick. Shit, shit, shit. Thick, thick, thick."

My eyes lighted from Nancy to the fat blonde boy who was now spitting on himself to the pink-haired girl to the other little boys and I marveled at the tic orchestra, so amazed by the variation in movements and gestures and sounds that I forgot about my own repertoire. Parents, mostly moms, took turns talking to Glen and each other about their kids being bullied and placement in Special Ed classes and Clonidine patches versus herbal remedies but I sat silently, never joining in the conversation. I happily tic watched.

At one point, I could tell the pink-haired girl was imitating my wrist popping. I purposely touched my head. She did, too. "Simple Simon," I thought. I reached up to scratch my scalp. She did to and she noticed me noticing her and she blurted out, "It's echopraxia."

"Echo what?" I said.

"Echopraxia," she repeated. "It's when you imitate other people's actions. I have echolalia, too," she explained. "That's when you repeat what people say."

"Eat shit and die, you fuckin' bitch!" I said, in order to test her claims.

Instead of echoing me, the girl said, "Thanks."

"Glen," started the peeved father of the poor five-year-old redhead beside me. The fucker was obviously French and had a mad superiority complex. He repeated, "Glen, eh, do you sink zees," he pointed at his son's jerking neck, "can be caused by estress? Een France, vee don have as mash stress. Perhaps putting zee boy in a new environment veel help? Or a vacation in the countryside?"

Nancy and her mom looked at each other like, "Motherfucker has got a lot to learn."

Glen clicked into lecture mode. "Sir, your son has tics. So his neck jerks a little. It's not caused by stress and a vacation's not gonna make it magically disappear."

Nancy nodded. "I'll keep my tics any day," she said. "Just take my OCD."

Glen pointed at her. "See. It's the things you can't see that torture. So the boy moves his head. It's something you can learn to live with."

The Frenchman didn't appreciate the new asshole he'd been torn, but even I knew he deserved it. Trying to get all high and mighty on us like in France none of this shit happens. Didn't he catch the name of the damn disease? Tourette? Its discoverer's first name was Gilles, for chrissakes. The Frenchie stewed, his nostrils flaring, and to add insult to injury, his wee fidgeter snorted a bad-ass "Oink."

Glen looked at the wall clock. Four o'clock.

"Well, we've gotta vacate now," he announced. "Please, take any of the leftovers." He gestured at a refreshment table that held half-empty cookie trays and juice boxes on ice. "The oatmeal are delicious, today," he added.

A kid in a scout uniform walked backwards to the snacks and stopped when he bumped into the table. His mom stared at him. "That's a new one," I heard her mumble.

I felt a hand touch my shoulder. I turned. The pink-haired girl.

"You're a teacher!" she said. "How old are you?"

"Twenty-two."

"Wow! You look, like, fifteen. You must have good genes."

"Not that good," I said. "Otherwise, I wouldn't be here."

"Ha, ha!" She sized me up, taking in my formfitting Liberace t-shirt, black leather miniskirt, leopard-print creepers. "You've got good taste, too."

"Thanks," I said. I thought I should offer her a compliment. "I like your hair."

"Thanks. I have a hair dying tic. I change the color about once a week. Where are you going?"

"Home."

"So am I! Where do you live?"

"Telegraph and Alcatraz."

"Really? That's on my way home. Wanna ride the bus together?"

"Sure."

Me and the enthusiastic pink-haired girl left First Presbyterian together, and watching her skip, twirl, and reach down to touch the ground, I felt like a novice clumsily following a master. We caught the bus in front of a bakery where Rae almost got mugged one night and shared a seat. I ignored the familiar scenery, the Thai and Ethiopian restaurants, the auction house, a fortuneteller's with a crystal ball in the window.

"That's so cool that you're a teacher," the pink-haired girl said, and I realized I didn't know her name. "What do you teach?"

"English. To grown-ups." My head shook back and forth vigorously, rattling my brain.

"Is that a tic?"

Dizzy, I nodded. "What's your name?" I asked.

"Freya."

"Freya?"

"Yeah. Not what you expected, huh?"

I shook my head. Not a tic.

"Freya's a—"

"—Norse goddess," I finished. "It's a Scandinavian name."

"How'd you know?"

"My dad's a linguist."

"My step-dad's a lawyer."

"Is one of your parent's white?" I hazarded to ask.

"Yeah. My real dad. My mom's Japanese. I came out looking really chinky." Freya grabbed the corners of her eyes and pulled them back, exaggerating their slant. Then she pointed at her cheeks. "Look! I've got white girl freckles!"

I looked. She did. I studied all of her face, noticing how pretty and delicate she was. Her eyes were rimmed with kohl. Her lips were thin and her nose had breakable, porcelain nostrils.

"What grade are you in?" I asked Freya.

"Twelfth. I'm a super senior. I love school. I'm turning eighteen this month and I still won't graduate for another year."

"How come?"

"I'm credit deficient. I hated my old teacher so I used to ditch all the time. But the new E.D. teacher is cool. I like her.

"What's E.D.?"

"Emotionally disturbed. That's the class I'm in. It's all kids who can't sit still or give their teachers a hard time or don't ever do their homework. I'm the only girl in the class. I get a lot of attention."

"You go to Berkeley Classical?"

Freya nodded.

I pulled the string to ding the bell. We were at our stop. I turned to her.

"Are you coming?"

"Sure," she said.

I led us off the bus and heard the white heels of Freya's go-go boots click against the floor behind me. We clattered down the steps and walked past the gas station to my apartment building. I took out my keys to open the gate but put them away. The door was already propped open by a stack of phone books.

"Come on," I said.

Freya followed me through the small courtyard, up the stairs of my complex, which looks a little like a ski lodge, and huddled on my worn doormat was El Tecolote, holding a dozen long stemmed roses in one hand, a bottle of champagne in the other. Impatience was written all over his face but when he saw me, he lit up.

"Meez Garcia," he said in English. "I bring for you geeft."

"You already gave me a gift," I reminded him. "The poem. At my birthday party."

"Dees eez my real geeft."

"How do you know where I live?" I demanded.

"La quiero[68]," he answered.

"Tecolote. Soy lesbiana[69]."

---

68   I love you.

69   I am a lesbian.

"No," he said adamantly. "Joo are too bootiful."

"Soy lesbiana."

"Tu novia[70]?" he nodded at Freya.

I didn't answer.

"Esta fea[71]," he said.

El Tecolote had gone to the wrong place. Freya was good. Freya was genuine and naive and honest. At her tender age, she had the balls to wear a craziness on her sleeve that I'd tried to kill and bury and hide and suffocate. Fuck E.T. I got dizzy. Just from pure anger. I felt hooting and fuck yous building up in my vocal chords, and punches and kicks in my limbs.

"Fea," he repeated and pulled the trigger in my brain.

I barked like a seal and rolled my eyes back in my head and bit so hard at the air that I felt a tooth crack. I knocked E.T.'s crutches out from under his arms and blew a raspberry in his face. Then I slapped him.

Stunned, but without any major physical impairment, E.T. leaned over and picked up his crutches. His roses were all over the ground, petals smashed. The champagne bottle had fallen too, but miraculously it was unbroken. With his crutches tucked below his arm, he cried, "Pinche marimacha loca!" and stormed down the wood stairs, taking them two by two, sailing out the front gate.

Freya ticced, "Pinche marimacha loca!" in a Smurfette voice. "What does that mean?"

"Fucking crazy dyke."

"Oh," she said, unphased. "Look," she pointed with the toe of her shoe. "The bottle's fine."

"I know," I said. "Come on in. I think I have some ice in the freezer inside."

---

70   Your girlfriend?
71   She's ugly.

Tit for Tat

This morning, I put on my new favorite t-shirt. Rae got it for me for my birthday from Planet Consignment, which is billed as "an upscale thrift store." This new shirt's got perfect symmetry, it's white with black letters, and the letters say "Tit for Tat" across the chest, one noun on either boob, a preposition in between. It's too perfect.

I wore the shirt to San Francisco with Freya. We took the BART there and hung out at the shops around Union Square. Then we hiked up to FAO Schwarz to play with all the display toys and went dumpster diving behind the Sanrio store, looking for defective Hello Kitty merchandise. We found plenty and loaded it into our purses like pillaged pirate's booty.

Knee deep in garbage, I'd justified my dumpster diving to my OCD this way: I won't get sick exposed to all the germs and funk living in the trash because the universe knows my rooting around in it is a noble act.

I'm saving things. I'm resurrecting them from an early grave. Seeing perfectly good junk being tossed out gives me anxiety and I feel like I'm watching things be buried alive. My rational side, however, recognizes the erroneousness of these thoughts. Hoarding is yet another symptom of OCD and everyone knows a hoarder, an old woman whose house overflows with cats, a man whose car is packed with crushed paper cups, used rubber gloves, cigarette butts.

I'll need to stop salvaging unless I want my home to end up like Langley Collyer's, America's most notorious hoarder. In 1947, amid stacks of newspapers stretching back to 1915, police serving a warrant at his Harlem apartment found an impressive collection of useless things: a Metropolitan Opera program from 1914, a Model-T, Langley's brother Homer's corpse.

I got home around five and unpacked my new toys and set them on a living room shelf. I was yawning when Mom called, but I talked to her anyways. I could tell she had something big to tell me and when she asked "You know what?" I knew she was finally going to cut to the chase.

"What?" I asked.

"Fe is getting divorced. Eusebio was having an affair. Can you believe that?"

I recalled my uncle's roving eyes.

"Yes."

"And your cousin Nito is getting married." Mom went silent, pausing for dramatic effect. "His girlfriend already had their baby, though. A girl. Guess what they called her?"

"I don't know."

"Desiree."

"That's disgusting, Mommy."

"I knew you would say that."

"Well, it's true," I argued. "That's just crummy."

"I knew you would say that," Mom said. "I knew you would say precisely that."

I smiled, "Did you?"

"Yes. I did. I knew you would, mija.[72]"

The word didn't sit right. "Mommy," I purred slowly, "can you say mija again, please?"

"Ay, Desiree. Why?"

"Because. I need to hear you say it."

"Mija."

"Again?"

"Mija."

"Again?"

"Mija!"

"Okay. That was good."

"Desiree…"

"I know, Mommy, I know."

"Mija," she said again and giggled.

I moaned. We were going to have to start all over again.

---

72   my daughter

About the Author

Myriam Gurba was born in Santa Maria, a small, semi-rural California town located a stone's throw from Michael Jackson's Neverland Ranch. The daughter of well-educated Mexican immigrants, Gurba spent her early years as an unruly punk teenager and then as a sad gay Goth.

Diagnosed with both Obsessive-Compulsive Disorder and Tourette's Syndrome, Gurba still managed to graduate with honors and a BA in history from UC Berkeley. Her writing has appeared in many anthologies including *Best American Erotica* (St. Martin's), *Bottom's Up* (Soft Skull), *Secrets and Confidences* (Seal), and *Tough Girls* (Black Books).

Gurba currently resides in Long Beach, California, home of Snoop Dogg and the Queen Mary. This is her first book.